A Matter Of Time

by
Michael Crawford

A Matter Of Time
Copyright © 1997 Michael Crawford

ISBN: 1-893652-42-4

Library of Congress Catalog Card Number: 99-63986

This book was published using the on-line/on-demand publishing services of Writers Club Press.

405 N. Washington St.
Suite #104
Falls Church, VA 22046

URL: http://www.writersclub.com

CONTENTS

ACKNOWLEDGMENTS

In the mind of a beginning writer there is really nothing to be concerned about. One simply sits down at a keyboard and starts filling in the words to a story. Well, the story came to me at a Sam's Club one day in about forty five minutes from beginning to end. I did as I thought it should be done, I sat down at the keyboard and began to pour out the words. Oh, the idea was wonderful, the story was one that was waiting to be told, and in my own imaginations, it would be simple. WRONG! It was not until I was into the first section that I figured I should let some other's see what I was doing. I had no fears that it was anything less than perfect, after all this was my golden opportunity to be what I wanted to be, a writer. I quickly found out I'm glad I didn't select to become a brain surgeon.

Being on America On Line first gave me the first idea to write, so I went to others on AOL to seek their opinions. Well, I found out asking for opinions did get the results I had anticipated. The first person to read the work, told me how good I was, how I had captured the essence of the thinking of a woman, the passion of how they feel, the grander of the realm of possibility thinking, and that I was born to be a writer. Oh, how my chest inflated, my ego surged and my hopes leaped for joy. Naturally I continued to write more on the story. It was not until I presented it to the true friends on AOL that I got what I needed and what was the bitter truth about my work. There is a strange thing about friends, they aren't friends because they tell you what you want to hear. They tell you what you need to hear, and for that, I will forever be grateful. They are more than what some would consider friends. They were honest and in a way, saw the heart of the idea behind the story and simply out of love, wanted to advise me on where I had erred. I am going to list them, as best as I can in a chronological order, and hope I don't fail to leave neither a person, time or comment out.

The first person to see this, and perhaps the most important at the moment was Mary Jo. I do not have her permission to use her name, so her first name will have to do. She was the kind one. She was the one that perhaps saw my fragile ego was not to be disturbed with formalities like verb tense, and other obvious mistakes. Perhaps she never really knew that by her first comments, I would go on to finish the book, after all, she only got the first section. Mary Jo, thank you for being the first friend to see that there was possibilities there.

My first encounter with a real friend was Linda Eaton, otherwise known as Shanna. She was most diplomatic, but because she saw more to the story, and perhaps me, she was honest, candid, and spoke up about my most obvious misuse of grammar. It was Linda that introduced me to the great number of shortcoming as a writer that I would have to endure. Linda, for your kindness I can't express in words the gratefulness I truly feel. Thanks for the long hours of editing at night, along with all the conversations on line. I truly feel I personally know David and Adam.

As I began to give the story to more people, you would know the next person was, by choice not by profession, an editor. She loved the story and cared for me personally or else she would not have been so blunt. Annie Jacs was God sent. She taught me to use words in the proper way and apply them in the most correct manner. Annie, you will never know the degree I loved you showing me how much I had forgotten from all the wasted time in English classes. Ms. Loftin always wanted me to broaden my horizens, yet I think she would have also appreciated the correct tense.

The story, in and of itself, was in part, how a woman felt. I was compelled to see if my meager interpretation was right. I started to send it to several woman on line. I had a target reader in mind, but wanted to know what was felt in the general attitude. It was at this time that I got back to my Mary Jo types that gave me just what I needed, not correction of grammar but, the truth about how women felt and how they would look at the situation Maggie would truly be living. It was only as I received their comments that I understood that my perception was in part right. I say in part for each of them had an opinion of what they felt and shared. Each one will never know that it was their input which made me see in which direction I should begin to flow.

I first met Pamela S. Hayward by accident and it was one of the best moments of my life. She was a single mother, with a pre-teen daughter (what else can I say) that showed me women were much more than I had ever dreamt them to be. She did not only encourage me to write, but she put me on her web page. She extended to me something I had not known. She saw in me more that perchance I did not see in myself, and gambled on my work in her home page. Little did she know I had much to learn about the English language. Pam thank you for simply being the most kind and gentle person you have always been. Those little things you do in life do come back like the bread on the water. A smile comes to my face when I consider another that brought joy to me about this time in the book.

I was very fortunate to meet several humanitarian women in the form of nurses. These have seen a degree of disappointment and sorrow that conceivably others have not been blessed. Nurse Julia was the first, and over the months was one that I began to realize I had touched, but for the first time in a real manner. Until then, it had only been a thought in my mind, never realizing it could actually be real in some lives. Julia, thank you for simply opening up to me with your honesty and sometimes very painful reality. And there was MartaRn, who was also very special. She endured much of what a woman must, and yet smiled at the simple possibilities of what simply lay ahead. She even allowed me to tell her separate stories, and complimented me on my hitting the "nail on the head". Marta, thank you so much for all you have done, and all the accomplishment I know you will achieve. And the nurse that taught me perhaps the most was Jamilah. She too is a writer and we spent many hours discussing agents, publishing and the like. We also shared on a personal level. Jamilah's insight is almost frightening, and her wisdom astonishing. If she ever tells you to check your truck before you go on a trip, do it. Thank you my special friend Jamilah for everything, particularly your friendship.

Then for the pure fun of it, I was pleasured to meet several others that simply brought me joy in their response. Some just thought I was being fresh, some thought I was being a gentleman, and some just enjoyed the sharing. Alice Domey was a real sport. It was in the getting to know her that showed me a great deal about women, and there is always a great deal to know.

She could laugh and cry about her situation. She could dream and then awaken to the reality of the moment. Alice your son will make it, simply because he has such a wonderful MOM.

Among the fun were several people that just simply were there for a delayed increasing of my ego. They were slow to read the work, and slow to answer back, but it was their views that made me see I had ultimately made my dream come true. Carolyn Herring is such a special person. Many morning while I was trying to work, and she was getting off from work, she game me encouragement with the fun and playfulness of a woman every man would enjoy. Thank you Carolyn for being the little girl in my life that continued to harass me because you thought I was naughty. I hope you continue, don't forget to take your medicine, you gave me hell one morning, and it endeared you to me.

Then there was Taviana Gerrato. She gave me hope in the first degree. She not only read my story, but she gave it to several other people. That was a very big statement in itself, and for that I will always be most appreciative. She did for a writer what most could never realize is important. She thought enough of it to share it, and that says a lot for her. You will always be special Taviana, and tell your sister and mom hello.

And Lori Collins was the first to write. She took the longest to read it. Her life was full of being a woman, a mom, a friend, a wife and all else that she was expected to be. I gained a greater understanding of what a real woman is by knowing you. It's nice to have the comments of the depth of a woman who is truly living as her own self in the midst of what she might enjoy being instead. Go Girl

Then we have the wild and crazy women on line that I just felt compelled to send the story. Those were a great deal of fun. They were the ones that seemed to bring about the last bit of mass encouragement I needed to continue to the end. The story had been finished, yet not edited, to the degree it has been done now, and yet they were just there. They were the writers of love stories, poems, and moments of the real heart they not only felt but lived. Sandra Brock, how I treasure your life. You seem to call out, "Thank you for understanding me." and that makes me feel good that I was pleasured by the moments you found your-self in reading my work. And then again, there was crazy Mary Roller Brosnan, what a morning woman. At a time when most would need several cups of coffee, she could hold her own against the best of them. Hell, in the morning, she was the best of them, thanks MR. And of course there was Leigh Chabot, a woman among women. Talk about not taking no bull. There was always a moment that one realized she was one that didn't get away. She was so straight forward that a fisherman would throw her back on purpose because he was not man enough to handle her. MAC you are mostly a friend.

Ahhhh, then there are those that one remembers just because they don't . By that I mean they don't pretend, they don't fake, they don't call anything less than what they see it, and that is a most welcomed change from time to time. There are three most remembered ones in the Author's Lounge that bring about a fun part of trying to accomplish something. They on the other hand, just bring you back to reality in the most fun way. Aimee Currie, known as Trixstar is one that simply makes you feel good about feeling bad. Aimee, thank you for cheering me up when I felt down with you most kind greetings. And then there was Marlene, AKA Mmtjb that was there for the moments when I was not truly sure of what I thought I was doing, but she showed me that I could. Thanks Marlene, I needed it.

Geina Worden was among those that I appreciate for finally taking time to read the story. She was one that I thought would never have the opportunity, yet she surprised me and saw it through. Thanks Geina for the opportunity to know and appreciate you.

Then again there was Rachel-Ann Ely. She never was so sublime as to tell me the truth about her thoughts. Thanks you Rachel, only you know what I really needed at the time, and the truth was not among that, yet I knew your caring all the while. And there was the serious one to cross my path before I decided to publish this book, Valary L. Johnson. Now she was something! She was not one to call a spade as a spade, she hand a tendency to call it a freaking shovel to the most brutal of degrees, but I truly loved that about her. I want you to know that now all I feel is the most humble of appreciation. Now, comes about Linda A. Fields. I some times have to laugh out loud at her extreme scrutiny of the book. It's extremely gratifing when one remembers so vividly my "nosing around" with the female feelings. I continue to smile when I see she is in the room, Thank you Linda for all the smiles and your help. And there was Victoria Cotton, from California. A mother, that was gathering a deep appreciation of being just that, a mother with the joy that brings, in spite of also being a woman. Such depth she gave me to realize that woman are special, and we as men sometimes never realize the devotion a mother shares.

And there was the Susan's. My sister's name is Susan and she didn't read the story, so for some strange reason I felt compelled to get a Susan's opinion. Susan Rosenbaum taught me great deal about how the Maggie's of the world felt. We could talk about most anything and all the while I was absorbing what the female perspective was about. She is a wonderful wife, devoted mother and she looks after the nursery at church and substitutes at school, now what more can be asked of her. Thanks Susan from all your contributions.

Last but by most certain measures is the person that had a dream. Deborah Shelton touched me by having the guts to be honest and tell me, after all the work which had been done, there was still a few mistakes. I will never forget when I ask her on what page, she said "Page One" and I shrank in total dispare. She just laughed and assured me that was her job. She was another God sent to me, and a true Saint in the utmost of words. I loved how she made corrections even on the parts that made her blush. Oh my Deborah, I love your innocent caring. Deborah put forth long hours in helping me. She helped do more than correct the errors of my work, she helped me know I could do what I sat my mind to, thank you so very much Deborah.

There are those I can't recognize. Those that also had a major part in the unfolding of this story for one reason or several. To them, and they know who they are, I extend my most heart felt gratitude. I was truly surprised at the number of women that saw through the fiction to grasp the reality. I'm especially proud to coin a word or an annacronym, "OILY" and, it is with the deepest of appreciation that I express a big **OILY** to ALL of the people that made my dream come true. It's not something that I ever realized I could do, but in realization I could not have done with out each and every one of you. As a man, I wish to express how much I truly appreciate your being the women that stand tall.

Introduction

One thing which will assist in the full understanding of this story is it has several portions written to invoke each reader to become one or perhaps both of the main characters involved. It is also intended to stir empathy with each character, as it may be pertinent to the reader. There are several themes allowing an opportunity for the reader to imagine the position of each character as if that position were real, and in many cases the odds of such an occurrence are most probable, as the idea of the circumstances came from observations of everyday life and human emotions.

Although the story only involves two individuals, which happen to be a male and female, it could also very well apply to a number of conditions as wide and as open as a phantasm of the mind and illusions of make-believe. Such an event has happened in the past and will most likely occur again in the future. If you believe long enough, hard enough, real enough, it could also happen to you in A Matter of Time.

THE MAN

There was a strange silence as the meeting began. For too many years now, every business associate he had ever had knew he was a man who generally got exactly what he wanted. Today was different. For the first time, it was as if he lacked interest, but no man at the table was going to do more than think this to himself. Over the years he had shown them he was extremely kind, generous and understanding. He built mutual respect on those attributes. Something was wrong today; they all felt its presence. He liked to walk around as he talked; even this usual trait was somehow just not there. Only the new guys were unaware that when he shifted his weight to one leg, he was in deep concentration or, when he put his hand to his head he was unsure. This was something only time taught. Those who were impatient soon learned the value of waiting. Those familiar with him, knew that the way he focused his eyes told them enough about him at the moment. It was something about his concentration, the deep prolonged glances that alerted those familiar with him that it was not time to talk, but to listen, and to listen very carefully to every word. The new guys would have to learn the hard way. Those who knew him loved him, for they had felt his love for them in ways that were hard to describe. It is a strange feeling when one knows something is wrong with a friend and helpless to lend a hand.

He had become a self-made man. His youth was not a

pleasant one. He was determined to be something more than his family had preconceived. He attended college as a self-imposed effort to get ahead, not for what the standards were intended. There had always been a dream in his mind, but he did not recognize it until he reached his middle twenties. It was then that he was transplanted from the deep south of Georgia to the northern shores of Maryland. He never lost the southern drawl, which had become so comfortable. He was driven to save money not really knowing why. He quickly found out when his first opportunity came. Fortune shined on him, even though his arrogance, ignorance and impatience fought against him. Not much time passed before he saw what he was fast to become. Several things, however, got in the way.

She was pretty, charming and most importantly, she was his father's choice. She would bring him into the real world his father thought he was overdue to enter. The effort was there, and sweet dreams of marriage soon left him empty. He never knew the reason; it was just another mistake he learned to endure. He quickly found himself returning to his prior self. He soon realized his life was void of what he truly wanted. His mind sought to find the answers, while at the same time, keep the goals he had previously set. For hours he would sit in solitude convincing himself that his goals would be realized. He was not uncomfortable with the thought that it would simply take time.

As his thoughts began to seriously focus on what he wanted, he brought himself closer to the answers. He almost instinctively knew when she appeared that she held the answers to his questions. It was there all the time, yet he was far too busy to stop long enough to see its simplicity. Michael absorbed everything and most of his life changed — the things he could change anyway. Others, such as previous mistakes, he lived with because he was an honorable man. He had been given a gift that he learned to utilize well. Now, despite fate, it was time to act on the requirement he knew would present itself in time.

She came to him in a way he was not accustomed, but when she boldly approached the table and stared into his eyes, she knew what he had secretly been seeking. For whatever reason, he knew she knew. He never got to know her the way he might have enjoyed, she simply introduced herself, said she had something he had wanted, and handed him an envelope. Their eyes never parted as she began to explain that what was in his hand would change his life forever. Normality was out of the question for him as her words sank deeply into his mind. There was a calm inside his soul that the answers he had longed for were to be revealed in the contents of the envelope. She walked out the door, but not out of his life. He soon learned to focus on her attributes, and would remember them for the future, for someday it would be his turn to do the same.

THE WOMAN

Her name is Margaret, but everyone calls her Maggie. The name has followed her from childhood. Her age has no significant importance. She is married, has two children, and has been employed long enough to become extremely bored with work.

She missed fixing breakfast for the family. The kids were nearly grown, her husband had changed his eating habits, among other things, and she was always late for work anyway. Perhaps it was the missing of the past that made her stop and think. Had things changed so quickly, or had she just failed to see them? Regardless of the reason, she was in a world of her own; one of herself with little consideration for anything else. Very little consideration had been given to her over the years it seemed, so she took the task on with pleasure.

Over the years, her life seemed to have a purpose. There was always something demanding her attention, yet she had failed to pay attention to the greatest one of all — herself. She cheerfully fulfilled the duties of wife and mother. It kept her mind, body and thoughts busy. When the children were old enough to no longer need her constant attention, she took a job hoping it would not only bring in more money, but also give her a challenge. It was not easy being one person on the inside and acting like another on the outside. She would only pretend, for the aspirations she had once clung to were fading slowly away, if they had not already gone. It might have been a question of personal definition. The crystal clear ideas and ideals were now only a distant memory, but she would not and could not let them go. They seemed to be the only thing left to hold of what she knew to be herself; the self who had disappeared in the rush of life and the requirements of duty.

A young girl's conception of love, passion and romance quickly vanished. The real world seized control, like it or not. She found it rather ironic; she was a sales coordinator for a large public relations firm. She was very good at her job, yet wondered why she failed at coordinating her own life. She loved her family, but she felt taken for granted, as if she was there and always would be. Perhaps this is what she disdained most of all. She knew that concept was most likely true, but she didn't like it and longed to simply be appreciated, loved and in love. She could dream and no one was going to take her dreams away.

THE GROCERY

Over-the-hump day was yesterday, and it was like the week was starting over on Thursday. She felt like she had just pulled a double shift, yet not achieved one thing. As she exited the door on her way to the parking lot, she swore under her breath and vowed to only think pleasant thoughts. With this idea in mind, she noticed a long gray car parked on the roadside. She had often fantasized the man of her dreams would some day come in a limousine and whisk her away. Away from what was not totally clear in her mind. It was unusual that any car would be parked there, at this time of day.

Where exactly was she? she wondered, as she thought about that warm feeling of knowing you were cared about, satisfied, secure and wanted by the man in the gray car. Her gait slowed some as she thought about the feeling she remembered so well as if it were only yesterday, but in reality it was years ago, in her youth. Her husband had once sparked the yearning, and now it is only a fleeting daydream fantasy. What was it she was going to do after work today? She thinks to herself, not one of her favorites either, the supermarket for a few groceries. Seemed like once a week shopping didn't cut it with teenagers in the house now.

At last in her car, pulling out of the parking lot, she takes one last glance toward the gray car. It was gone. She thought to herself, back to the real world. Traffic was just as she, and the radio had predicted — slow; forty-five minutes later she got out of her car in the parking lot at the newly opened chain grocery. Full to the brim again. Her spot was the last in the far aisle back. Yeah, the walk'll do me good, right, she thought as she trekked toward the electronic doors. With her luck, they were broken tonight. As she reached the end of her row of cars, she was compelled to look back to her right and there it was again. That damned gray car, she thought. Fantasy was gone, but the car was there shining like a new dime.

Without even stopping to check prices, she instinctively pulled the most needed items from the shelf, then pulled back the reins to a dead stop. All at once, she felt as if she were the center of attention. There was a strange feeling as if her soul had just been touched in a most unusual way. Her eyes quickly used their natural radar and she found herself eye to eye with a tall man in a gray pinstriped suit. For a brief moment, it was almost as if each of them wanted to speak to each other, but there was just eye contact. Quickly each of them glanced in another direction, never acknowledging the other, and pushed their carts slowly away. She wanted to look back, but something told her not to, out of fear he might be looking back at the same time. From the corner of her eye, she noticed that he was resting his weight on one leg as he tried to look engrossed in the shelf. The edges of her lips began to curl with a half smile, wondering what he was thinking. She could enjoy the feeling one more time as they passed again on another aisle. This time each was overly cautious not to let the other know of the interest each one had generated. Even though they were very careful to pretend each went unnoticed, there was the transference of their thoughts. There was an unexplained knowledge of the other's presence. Silently, each was very aware of the other's mental attention. Finally, he disappeared.

It was time for the dreaded checkout line. She was not

going to be disappointed with the length of the line. When she was in a hurry, they all never failed to be long and slow. She just took her place in the shortest one she could find and started fumbling through her purse looking for her checkbook.

She had nothing to do but stand there, realizing she had chosen the slowest cashier on the planet. She was too afraid to move again, to a shorter line, when she saw him, pushing his cart on the farthest aisle from her. Now what? she thought, as he began to move past shorter lines on his way toward her. She had to admit he was handsome in the gray pinstriped suit. It was obvious he was some sort of businessman, well-bred, and from the items in his cart, which she had already observed in an effort to look away from his eyes, had good taste. But why is he passing up those lines to come over here in the snail's pace line? she wondered. She took note of his graying hair and his blue shirt and pinstripes, which caused a shine to his blue eyes, which were easily captivating. She then realized he was pushing his cart past the shorter lines to move toward her. She thought maybe he would stop at one of the other shorter cashier lines, but he did not. Now, he was behind Maggie. Her heart was beating just a bit faster for reasons unknown to her. For just a moment the silence between them was deafening, when he spoke. "I'm sorry to interrupt you," he said, with a broken southern accent.

As she was about to speak, just a millisecond later, she replied, "That's all right, looks like we will be in this line for awhile." Then, without thinking, and totally out of her normal character, she heard her voice say, "Why didn't you get in one of the shorter lines over there?" motioning with her hand to the location she was speaking about.

He replied quickly with the start of a mischievous grin on his lips. "That's a very good question, the best question you could have asked. It was because I wanted to speak with you personally. You see, I have admired you from the moment you first walked through the doors." He hoped the look in his eyes would not reveal the truth, he had in fact seen her many times, yet this was the first time he had engaged in conversation with her.

As he stood gazing into her eyes, the thought came to him that she was everything he had taken so long to conceive. For just a moment he wanted to become lost in her eyes. He took in a long deep breath and just looked at her, waiting for her response.

She was going to disappoint him, for his words had taken her temporarily off her guard. The compliment took away her breath and she was not nearly prepared to reply. What was going on here? She just hoped to God that no one noticed her reaction.

He continued in a lower, much softer voice, as if he were apologetic. "Please forgive the rather crude introduction. I must admit to you, as well as to myself, I have never done such an impulsive thing in my life, but it is my best mannered approach to introduce myself."

Again, his words brought about an unusual feeling of warmth. She wondered when she would have to reply and if she was ready, but he continued to speak.

"My name is Michael and, you look like a Martha to me," he said as he brushed his hand across the back of his hair.

"You're close, it starts with an 'M'," she said, just teasing him to inquire more about her. Then realizing he may actually ask for her name she continued. "I've never seen you in this store before. Are you new to this area or just visiting?" she asked really wanting to know the answers to many more questions.

The line started to move a few steps closer to the cashier, and his next question totally astonished her. His eyes looked more directly and deeply into her eyes as he said, "I would very much appreciate the opportunity to share a glass of wine with you, if you will?"

Her thoughts were those of mixed emotions. One side thought what the hell...? Can't you see this ring? I've worn it for eighteen years now. Who do you think you are? While on the other hand, she thought, Why do you make my heart race this way? Thank God she was quick on her feet. Without wanting to offend, or discourage him, she simply said, "Why, you don't even know me!" Quickly she put the ball back in his court, giving her time to compose herself for whatever his next question might be.

He said in his continued soft tone, "I told you in a small way awhile ago, and after all, this is a trifle bit on the personal side to discuss here. May I walk you to your car?"

The cashier began ringing up her items and she found herself saying, "Very well, if you wish."

This was not the reply she would normally answer. Now she was forced to confront him again in the parking lot. She thought to herself, What am I doing? I should have said no. But for some strange reason it was not what she wanted to say. The time spent checking those groceries was the longest five minutes of her life. She found herself waiting on him to finish with his items. She couldn't help but catch a glimpse of herself in a display rack mirror. Her assets far outshined her liabilities. Her complexion was smooth, her eyes bright and alive, and her body one that shows the efforts of every exercise to keep it looking good. That's why he wants to buy me a drink, she thought.

He picked up both of their bags of groceries, and followed her out the door to her car. Walking up the aisle, he paused and asked to be excused while he put his groceries in his car. What? To her surprise and amazement, it was once again the gray car.

"Now, exactly why did you want to walk me to my car and talk to me?" Maggie asked, with more authority and determination in her voice, but hoping not to be too demanding.

With gathered thoughts, he replied with the start of a mischievous grin on his face, "Do you honestly want to know everything, here and now? I can't help but be brutally honest. Besides it is the only thing which will work effectively with such a small time frame."

Starting to smile herself, in a coy way she replied, "And?"

With a much more serious tone, he replied, "Something just happened in the store. I cannot explain with any form of ration or reason to justify my actions, and to be frank, I am as nervous as a schoolboy, which is most uncommon for me. It is highly unlike me, but for the first time, in a long time, I fear your rejection."

There was a change in his voice telling her he was speaking the truth. Something she was waiting to hear for some reason. He continued much bolder now.

"I am married, have two children, own a successful business, and am filled with an overwhelming desire to hold you close to me. I will understand if you immediately reject this proposal or even slap my face for even conceiving such a notion, for at least I would be touched and get what I damned well deserve."

She didn't take time to think. "Very well, you have intrigued me," she found herself saying, as if she had done this a thousand times. "Wait, what am I saying?" she exclaimed. "This is not me and, as we are being honest, I thought my words would come out completely different."

Michael detected an emotion he could not quite explain, but knew that if he lingered much longer, something would go wrong. He had not contemplated this and he only wanted to excuse himself as quickly as possible. For lack of anything else to say, his honesty took total control and brought him an idea, which could end this very awkward situation. He began to speak rapidly saying, "Whatever you say. I regret I let my heart and emotions get the better of me. I should never have started this silly little game in the first place." He turned to walk away. He knew what he had planned, down to the very last detail, but she would have to willingly participate. He could only lead her so far. Now, doing all he could do, it was her turn to act.

Maggie's very own emotions were as waves in a hurricane, and knowing time was running out she started to shout, but quickly regained composure and said, "No, don't. Don't go, I…would like to share a few moments with you very much."

Now it was her turn. For just a second she began to tremble. She thought about the many times that she had wanted this to happen in a very secret way. Only in her mind had she ever conceived such a notion, yet now it was in front of her and this time real. Noticing the quiver she quickly said, "It's not a silly little game. You were only reacting to what I was sending out, quite unknowingly of course." Her voice became much softer. "This Saturday would be a convenient time for me, say around two o'clock in the afternoon. Would Peaches at the Track be suitable with you, Michael? I believe was your name," she asked, almost totally regaining her composure.

A sigh of relief came over his face. "Then two o'clock at Peaches it is." He turned and started walking back to his gray car. Just then Michael remembered, turned and asked, "You never told me your name, only that it started with an 'M'," he said with an almost boyish grin.

She replied with that same half grin, "It's Maggie, and that's enough for now," she said, climbing inside the car with an extremely warm feeling making her glow.

What in God's name have I just done? she asked herself as she slowly drove home. Never in her wildest imagination could this be happening, much less to have set a date with a man to be waiting for her at a specific date, time and place. Maggie would never think of cheating. Yet from all the years of being taken for granted, doing for others, she desperately wanted to feel the forgotten feelings of passion, warmth, tenderness and desire. These things were almost faded to memory. Trying to be objective just wasn't working now. Oh, how she longed for someone to put her feelings as their number one priority. But, was she willing to pay the price of the guilt feelings she knew would be waiting?

"What the hell. This is Thursday. A lot can happen in two days!" She said out loud, thinking her husband and the kids would take care of all her free time this weekend. But, this was not to be the case and the surprises were just beginning.

The next day Maggie's husband informed her his brother was doing some work and just had to have his help, experience and labor to finish on his home remodeling project. He said he was also going to take the kids. Their son could help with the work and his niece wanted to see their daughter.

They would be leaving early Saturday morning, spend the night and return late Sunday afternoon. She was invited, but his sister-in-law was out of town helping her mother while she recovered from surgery, so why would she want to come anyway? Great just throw me into Michael's arms! she thought, but in reality nothing else had occupied her mind since Thursday night. Now it was real. No excuses and the choices were to go or not go. All Maggie could think about was what she was going to wear. So many conflicting thoughts scrambled her mind. She was so totally thankful she had the forethought to set the date on Saturday when the work week crowd would be gone, and the time was past the usual lunch hour. Peach was a downtown restaurant and the chance of someone seeing her was very slim. Now, would she go? Would her guilt make her deny herself?

It was early Saturday morning and she had just seen her husband and kids off. She began to think about the day. As if she had all the time in the world, she did her usual chores. It was getting late in the morning. She knew it would take a long time to shower, put on her make-up, and she would definitely take longer than usual deciding on just the right clothes to wear, or not to wear. Again the feeling of what in God's name am I doing, came to the forefront of her mind. She was fully aware of what might happen, or it is better stated what she wanted to happen, and she wanted to be fully prepared.

She had recently bought a soft beige outfit, which was perfect. It complimented her hair and complexion. She knew what she thought about it and that was enough. If she were pleased, she's the only one who counted. This was her day, her fantasy and her reward.

The air was a bit cool, and she would have to wear a jacket. No one would notice or ever suspect she was without underwear. She would put some in her purse for later if needed. If she were going to live with danger, she was going to feel dangerous. She applied her make-up with a bit more care than usual. Her hair was her most desirable feminine feature and would get her the utmost of attention. Now, it's just an hour to go and suddenly, Oh no! I've forgotten what he looks like! She frantically searched every memory bank in her mind. Then she remembered. How she could possibly forget his blue eyes, as they seemed to look deeply into her soul and even beyond to her private imaginations? She calmed down, her heart and breathing slowed and she took time to notice the clock, one hour left. The ride would not be long; she knew her exact route and just wondered whether to arrive a tad early or a bit late.

Time took care of itself, exactly at two o'clock she walked through the doors at Peaches. She quickly spotted Michael in the back left-hand corner. He rose from his chair as she entered the door. She walked past each table and pretended not to notice anyone. In truth, she had covered the entire room in seconds making sure that no one was there she knew. Upon approaching Michael, she remembered the scent of his cologne, not one you'd recognize, but one not easily forgotten either. As she moved closer, he lifted his arms out to her, took her hands, leaned forward kissing her cheek, and whispered, "Welcome, I'm glad you are here."

PEACHES

As Michael saw to Maggie's chair, it was obvious she was still checking out the room with sharp quick glances over the entire area. There were very few people there at the time, and it was easy to find the assurances she needed. "I would have taken the liberty of ordering a bottle of wine, but I had no idea what you liked," he said as he motioned for the server.

"Oh, I couldn't have decided either, right now. I only know red, white, and blush which is exactly what I am feeling now," she said with a girlish smile of innocence.

"Well then, what can I do to make you feel as comfortable as you would like to feel?" he asked. As the server arrived Michael continued, "Perhaps a cocktail would relax you. What might be your pleasure?" as he ordered a scotch on the rocks.

"Okay," Maggie said, "I'll have an Ambush please."

"That's a new one on me," Michael said.

She smiled, much more relaxed already and said, "Good, the bartender will know what it is, and believe me it really sets the mood today." She chuckled and thought she had one on Michael, who seemed to know about wine, while she alone knew about the drink. She smiled and cast one more glance around the room.

"Are you comfortable?" Michael asked, knowing what thoughts were now running through her mind.

"Yes, I was just thinking about your greeting kiss. It was very nice. I felt you had planned this, and it made me feel very special."

"You are very special!" Michael said. "You have no idea just how special you really are to me. There are things you may never know or realize, but you have been on my mind for quite a long time now."

Maggie could not have had any other words spoken to her that would have moved her emotions more. She felt her heart melt at his words as she took a long breath and said, "I thought you were the overly impulsive one at the store the other night. Impulsive and a long time, are at totally different ends of the spectrum," she said softly, as the server brought their order.

"That's a very attractive outfit you are wearing," he said, hardly noticing the clothes for looking deeply into her eyes. She knew she had been right about it. Tan brought out her complexion and the black trim complimented her dark eyes and hair.

"Thank you, I picked this one out especially for you." Her smiling face revealed to him she was right and he felt flattered.

Talk was limited to what part of town they lived in, the age of their children, and several other trivial things of little importance but not to an in-depth degree. They never even inquired or relinquished their last names, just some easy conversation to help each of them relax with the present situation. It was an awkward few moments for each of them. Michael took a deep breath and slowly let it out as he repositioned himself to be more comfortable.

"Maggie, since I first saw you in the store, you were all I have considered. You have filled my thoughts far too much, and as much as I sincerely wish us to be most honest and candid, I almost decided not to come." He was unaware that the glow from his eyes was again giving himself away as he said, "Such a position would make me so much more vulnerable to my own desires than I have allowed myself to become."

Maggie's mind stopped, as well as her breathing. To think she could excite this man with whatever she possessed, and loving every minute. She was strangely drawn to his passion, silently knowing and feeling his inward desires.

"Why I...I'm not sure what you are talking about," she said as if his words had gently slipped out of her mind.

Upon uttering those words, the look in his eyes and the tone of his voice changed. It was much more matter-of-fact, authoritarian, much more serious as he said, "We are adults. There's no need to pretend. If one is going to cheat, we should be brutally honest during these moments and not cheat ourselves as well." He paused a moment then continued. "This encounter is more than mere happenstance to me, you are more than just a pretty face I picked out to secure an afternoon of sexual pleasure." He stopped and noticed he had Maggie's full attention. "I could have afforded that with any one of several choices. It was you I chose and you I want."

Maggie started to speak but Michael looked into her dark eyes and motioned, "Wait, let me finish," and continued. "Of course you have the right to know more about me, and I will answer your questions, but you must also realize there are certain things, within this relationship, you will never know, and it is for your best interest they simply not be discussed. Now ask away my dear, Maggie." He politely smiled in his usual way, rubbed his head and continued to gaze into her eyes.

"Very well, my turn it seems," she smiled. "I appreciate your forthrightness, honesty and candor, and if this is what you truly want, I hope you can stand the heat, cause I'm lighting the match!" She looked away from Michael's eyes. Then, catching herself she simply said, "All right!"

"All right what?" Michael asked, catching her contagious grin.

Before Maggie had an opportunity to think, she found herself saying, "All right I want you too, I guess… Are you satisfied? You have me all confused and saying just what you want me to say," Maggie said in frustration.

"No, no Maggie, I can do a great many things, but put words into someone else's mouth is not one of them, my dear. You were saying your own thoughts and I merely stand in deep appreciation," he said with the smile Maggie was growing accustomed to seeing.

Caught totally off guard, and really not knowing what to say next for fear of what might come out next, accidentally or not, Maggie simply said, "Well, what do we do now? Next? Whatever?"

Michael's smile transformed into his unmistakable chuckle. He knew he had gotten his original point across and had Maggie in a state of confused bliss. Then, still laughing he said, "I would have asked you where and what you preferred, but I had the uncanny feeling you would be pleased if I make this decision, and I will. A friend of mine has a home on the lake not far from here. It would be my utmost pleasure to show it to you," he said.

His eyes sought her permission and Maggie nodded her head in a polite approving manner. Michael paid the check, took time to secure Maggie's car and helped her into his gray car.

"How long have you had this car Michael?" she asked.

"A few weeks, why?"

"Oh nothing," she said as she remembered small portions of when her fantasy first began.

For the first time in many years Maggie enjoyed watching Michael care for her car and for her security. She noticed over the years the feeling of protection was instilled in her heart, but had somehow lost the feeling of romance she was feeling now with him. After he opened the door for her, and started the motor, the CD player came on with the most soothing music she had ever heard. After only going a few miles she felt at peace. Was it the alcohol, the music or the moment? She wondered as they drove.

"What do you do for a living, Michael?" she asked, just wanting to hear his voice again. "From your clothes, I assume you are involved in the business world, stocks, real estate. Am I close?"

"A bit!" He said. "I have several irons in the fire, never knowing when a trend will change and that iron is no longer prosperous, so I am open to change," Michael said. "And you work for Reynolds, Dunlap & Dyer, advertising firm as coordinator of sales promotions."

Maggie sat up straighter. "Yes, and how did you know this information?" She asked, as if the information were privileged.

"Maggie, I have actually known a great deal about you for some time not just since I met you in the store. When I was in Carl Dunlap's office several months ago, it was then that I first noticed you. Take it as flattery. Carl told me about you and admired my great taste." He pulled into a drive that led to a most elegant home overlooking the lake with a scenic mountain view as a backdrop.

Michael stopped the car and leaned over to kiss Maggie. The memories of the next few moments would be eternally etched in time. It was as if their movements had been flawlessly choreographed. Each seemed to have held back the tension as long as they possibly could. Their lips met and the tenderness of this first kiss was almost indescribable. Just moist enough to glide over the outer surfaces and hungrily thirst for more. Slowly their lips opened and eagerly searched for deeper treasures. The tip of Michael's tongue began to search Maggie's inner lips. Soon, she was caressing his lips in return. She had never cared for scotch whiskey before, but the lingering taste in Michael's mouth had immediately caused her to wonder why. Michael was captivated by the warm succulent taste, which was thrilling every fiber in his body. Knowing what was in store, in just the next few moments, each slowly withdrew and took their time recovering from the moment of bliss.

The cabin, as Michael called it, was something out of one of those glossy home magazines. To her surprise, everything was decorated as if it were a resort rental.

"Is this where you usually bring your mystery dates?" Maggie asked.

Michael turned with a completely different look in his eyes, and with a much greater sense of seriousness said, "This is a joint-venture rental property of which I own an interest, that's all. And", he continued, "I have never had any mystery dates in the past. This is a first time affair, if you wish to call it that, for me, and you must try to understand just how special you are to me." He turned toward the bar and quietly asked if she wanted anything to drink.

Maggie was moved by his sincere reply and felt compelled to be just as honest and up-front. And with her matter-of-fact tone of voice, she said, "Michael, let's agree on something up front. Whatever takes place is here and now, never again to be replayed. This is today, and tomorrow it will simply be a memory we shared yesterday. Agreed? If you can't agree with those terms, we should call this thing off, now!" Maggie said determinedly.

Michael took her in his arms, held her tenderly and whispered, "Agreed."

THE CABIN

"I'll give you the grand two-minute tour of the place," Michael said. "But, excuse me while I see about something for a minute," and he was gone.

Maggie walked over to the side of the cabin overlooking the lake. The entire A-frame wall was a giant window. The view was breathtaking. She wondered to herself, for about the two thousandth time if it were really her here, and not someone else who had escaped from inside her own body. Then the chill of cold feet began to come over her and she felt the smallest start of a shiver from guilt. Just then Michael was behind her and his arms encircled her waist holding her gently.

"What a marvelous view from this window. Can the people on the lake see inside?" Maggie asked, still wondering who might be on the lake.

"No, there is a special chemical treatment on both the inside and outside to secure total privacy. You see, when you are paying $1,000 per day for the very best, one expects every detail to be provided," he said as his arms moved up her back to the base of her neck. "Are you still comfortable?" he asked. He felt the small quiver of fear her body was displaying.

"Yes, but never having done this sort of thing before, I hope you understand my position," she said as his hands began to move up to the back of her head.

"I completely understand." Much more than you understand, he thought, for it is a first and only time for me. At last you have come and presented me with the greatest of all wishes.

"Would you do me a big favor? Close your eyes and take a deep breath," Michael whispered and she did as he requested. "Now, breathe out and keep your eyes shut. If it is of any comfort, my eyes are also closed," he said as his hands began to tenderly stroke her hair.

Without a word being spoken, Michael began to gently caress her head, her ears, cheekbones and mouth. His touch was soft, gentle and the lingering odor of his cologne remained on his hands. Maggie caught the slightest smell of the scent she recalled from the market. His hands continued to her chin, back to her neck and shoulders, causing her breathing to increase as her heart raced faster. Michael pulled back her long dark hair from her ear and almost inaudibly he whispered, "Still, very quietly, listen to the sound your mind and body are shouting."

With a firmer grasp, his hands moved down her arms to her hands, to touch each finger with an individual caress. She wondered which would happen first. Would her legs give way with weakness or her heart explode with excitement? Yet, still his hands never stopped their movement. Back on her shoulders, they began to descend down her back, fingers spread wide to capture the entire area. The tips spread a new tingle over her body as they slowed at the base of her spine and continued downward over the tight form of the bottom of her skirt. Michael again moved against her ear and moaned a sigh that let her know he was aware there was nothing between her skin and skirt.

Michael was very much aware of the effects of his movements on Maggie. Without wanting to rush the moment, he turned her around, looks for a second into those dark brown eyes, and with his long arms around her slender frame, held her tenderly next to him. There was no description of the joy he was experiencing. At last, he was filled with the knowledge that his energies had not failed. Just then an idea came to him and he paused his embrace, went over to the sofa and retrieved a small pillow and tossed it on the plush carpeted floor. He gently took Maggie's long slender hands and asked her if she would join him on the carpet in front of the tremendous glass wall. She was glad she wore her new tan outfit. She liked the feeling of the soft brush cotton top and matching skirt. Its movements reflected the way her heart was feeling, gently bouncing graciously with style.

"I wanted you to lie here with me for several reasons. First the view, as the sun starts it's decline from the sky, is extremely beautiful. And second, I want to take a few minutes to gaze into your eyes, and allow you the same opportunity, if you don't object," Michael said as he motioned downward.

Although she felt lying on the carpet was an unusual request, she agreed and her outfit made her grateful she had decided to pick this particular one. Michael gently took her hand and tenderly guided her to exactly where he wanted.

Making sure she was comfortable, Michael turned toward the kitchen and returned with two large wine glasses filled with a new wine he wanted Maggie to taste.

"I hope you will like this, I bought it on a suggestion, and wanted you to have it nearby, as I wish to ask another favor," he said as he lay down beside her and propped his head on his hand and arm.

Maggie thought for a moment. Why was she so willing to do as he asked? Why was his request so important to her? Yet, this was a minor point when her wishes were being so well fulfilled. As he continued.

For the next few moments they looked silently into each other's eyes. Without uttering a word, their thoughts just tranquilly mixed. She could feel his breathing and its rhythm relaxed her even more as she realized she was completely losing herself in pleasant thoughts of him with her own free will.

She willingly looked into his brilliant blue eyes, the one prominent feature, which had easily captivated her upon their first meeting. Eyes so intuitive and searching, she was at first reluctant to allow her eyes to totally meet his for any length of time. Doing so, she knew would allow him access to the inner core of her being she had granted no one entrance before.

As each second passed, Michael's gaze seemed to pierce deeper inside Maggie's thoughts, going past them even to the heart of her soul. He thought to himself as he concentrated on her returning gaze how fortunate he felt, to have worked on her image for such a long time and now have her lying beside him. Over a year ago, he had started planning this day, knowing it would come and yet he had not known just how perfect she would be in the flesh. Just then he closed his eyes and thought how he had longed for this feeling.

He married out of college to his father's best friend and

business partner's daughter, just to keep the correct social position. He and his wife loved each other, but somehow never quite fell in love. He would have done something, but the kids came along, his business grew, and he could never get up the courage and time it took to get a divorce. He truly loved his wife, yet had never fallen in love with her. It was the love that held him, and the not in love causing the emptiness in his heart.

With eyes still closed, Michael reached out for Maggie's hand, and wondered just how he could please her. For the first time in such a long time, the thought had entered his mind. Until then, it was his duty. There were so many things he wished to do to please her. He knew he wanted most just to touch her softly and instill this feeling in his memory. He opened his eyes and released Maggie's hand. He began to gently touch her face as her eyes stared back, his hand slid down to her neck and to the first button on her blouse. As his fingers slowly maneuvered the button, Maggie began a quiet smile, and gave her unspoken permission. After he had undone the first two buttons, Maggie closed her eyes and began to think to herself.

Her thoughts were strictly of herself. Why was she here? Why this man? Why had she not made an attempt to stop? Why did she want his touch so much? As she felt the second button release, she knew she had also released any and all inhibitions to stop what she had wondered about for the last two days. When was the last time her husband had showered her with this attention? When was the last time his passion had been given to her with tenderness and romance? She knew it had been needed, wanted, and would have been appreciated much more than words could ever express. Maggie loved her husband and family, but the situation had become one of being taken for granted and she wanted it replaced with

Michael's feelings, even for a just a moment of time to give her room to think. Thinking was now becoming difficult and she felt compelled to open her eyes.

In reality, the animation of Michael's movement caused her eyes to open, only to find his eyes closed, and his lips slowly descending toward her face. She closed her eyes and felt his soft lips tenderly touch hers and took a slow breath to capture the moment for memory, perhaps a memory that would have to last the rest of her lifetime. That was a thought that she didn't want to enter her mind. She quickly dismissed it as Michael's tongue danced over her lips; she parted them slowly, inviting him. He penetrated her mouth and for however slow that moment may have seemed, they were both transformed to a new plane of existence. Maggie felt Michael's hand as it tenderly surrounded her right breast, which responded almost instantaneously with a pebble hard nipple. The feeling of his hand sent a shiver over her entire body, even in the heat of the setting sun through the glass wall. Before she could recover from one sensation, he created another as his fingertips softly glided from her blouse, over her stomach, to the top of her skirt. Still involved in that long, now wet, kiss she almost broke the silence with a moan, but took a deep breath through her nose. Michael's fingers began to play with both her skin and the belt, but soon had it unfastened and was tickling her as he began to undo the one and only button. Both of their hearts were pounding loud enough to be heard inside and over their thoughts.

Maggie could no longer resist the temptation to reach out to Michael. With her right hand she moved upward and over to him as he moved his warm body. She had brushed against his firm muscle hardened leg, and her attention was quickly interrupted. Michael slowly unzipped her skirt. Her entire body was so tense, even with the small release of pressure, she felt as if she were free to take in more air with each breath. She was thinking, please, move faster in one second and stop right there, in another, but soon she felt his hand, fingers fully extended, begin to slip under the band of her skirt. She quickly tightened her grasp on Michael's leg only to find the muscle was not his leg. It was at this moment of realization; she was compelled to take in another breath as the tips of Michael's fingers now were tangled in the curly soft down of her pubic area. His touch was extremely tender and exciting. No longer could she simply lie there. She knew instantly upon his touch that she must move, and quickly placed her hand on the back of Michael's head and began to curl her fingers around his hair. Michael's hand stopped its downward movement and he began to rise from the floor.

As he began to untie his tie, he said quietly, "I might make a suggestion of another place, which may be much more comfortable. Would you like to see?" as he started to unbutton his shirt.

"Why Michael, I never thought you'd ask," Maggie said with a smile as she slipped out of her vest and skirt.

Standing there in front of each other, a moment of silence took place as their eyes met. Maggie was short and petite and weighed only about a hundred and twelve pounds. Michael bent down to her, put one arm around her waist and the other under her knees. The next moment she was lifted high in the air moving toward the bedroom door. Michael had turned down the bed covers and as he gently, as a soft cloud, lay her down, there was a coolness of the fresh crisp sheet against the heat of her body.

THE FULFILLMENT

For a moment each of them stopped all movement. There was a realization that neither of them had ever come this far. The slightest sensation of fear engulfed them at the same time. There was a silence and each respected the other's thoughts. Was there love there? Were they running away rather than toward something? Each had a personal concept, yet there was a sharing they both understood. This moment was a once in a lifetime experience. As they peered deeply into each other's eyes, an understanding was reached. They would not remember other experiences. This was to be anew. They would not bring with them the feelings that had been shared with anyone else. The knowledge of what was waiting was so much more than any previous moment. What they wanted would be done. What they desired would come true. This was a first and a last time, and they both encountered the same emotion at the same time. This was only their time. This was their world, and the world outside was, for the moment, nonexistent. There were no taboos.

Maggie's breathing seemed to increase with each step Michael took. In an effort to justify being there, she realized how no one had ever treated her so lovingly, tenderly and with so much respect. This is what she had longed for and desired in her fantasy. In a way she wanted for it to stop now, so it would always be remembered as perfect. Yet, her body cried out to continue, and as Michael slid his right arm from under her waist, her wish was fulfilled.

As he moved to be on her opposite side, he stopped directly over Maggie's body and looked deeply into her eyes, then descended to her waiting lips. For just a moment, each of them sensed, and felt, the other one tremble. Each of them knew this moment, for whatever reason, had been given to them to share. Such pleasure they were about to experience was their destiny, and to be remembered forever. As their kiss ended, Michael kissed her cheek, her neck and then the lobe of her ear as he whispered, "I have envisioned this moment for years, you are far more than my imagination could have created in my mind. You have given me a gift which could not be imagined in the mind, but you are here now, and I desire every part of you." He continued his kisses downward. By that time, Maggie was in what she thought was total euphoria, but the feeling would only continue to be more intense by the moment.

Michael's arms supported him. His head and mouth were forced to do his bidding. His soft lips kissed each of Maggie's breasts; first one then the other. As he continued encircling each one, he felt the tautness of her nipples against his cheek, and heard her heartbeat grow faster. With his teeth, he nibbled tenderly at each nipple until it reached its total erection. The coolness of the darkened bedroom chilled her from the moisture of his mouth, and Maggie closed her eyes. For a long while Michael continued to caress each breast with his mouth. He kissed every part with lips and tongue until Maggie thought she was going to scream. He stopped and continued slowly down her body.

Her hands reached out to touch him. Michael spoke softly, but quickly, "Please Maggie, my fantasies began days ago and I want this to last for me. The mere touch of your hand on me would excite me too much now and bring about something I could not control."

Maggie, knowing exactly what he was talking about, simply ran her fingers through his hair and enjoyed the feeling of his lips and tongue descending down her stomach. Her eyes closed again.

Maggie's body wanted to move upward in a quick jerk. Her imagination ran wild with expectation, and she prematurely enjoyed Michael's every move. Michael positioned his weight on his knees and, with each hand held Maggie's arms. Slowly he stroked them and then held her hands. His knees positioned him downward. The tension was extremely high, knowing what was about to happen. Michael's tongue was wet and warm as his kisses stopped short of her soft, curly, black down. Maggie took in a deep breath waited for his next move, which quickly began. With his nose he glided over the silkiness of her adornment surrounding her special place and released a breath directly onto her clit. With that, Maggie moaned and whispered, "Oh, Michael that sends chills up and down my body, my desire is reaching its' limits...." He squeezed her hand and continued his downward movements.

From side to side his tongue explored the lips that softly covered his desire. His decision on how to open them sent Maggie's body into spasms. He moved his head lower, but still allowed his nose to continue to touch her down. His tongue penetrated her inviting opening and he forced it to enter as deeply as he could. With that same movement, his nose recognized the firmness of Maggie's clit and pushed harder as he began his upward movement. By that time, Maggie had produced a continuing flow of clear, silky, warm fluid for which Michael used his tongue as a container to capture every amount possible and began his ascent.

Trying not to show her total excitement, Maggie made every effort to think of when the last time her husband bestowed this gift on her. Far too long, and never enough between the times, she needed to be granted this pleasure. Now, it was happening, her senses were almost at their peak and she was unable to think, just enjoy. For Michael had reached her longing clit with the tip of his tongue. Using the silky fluid he had brought with him from just down below, he glided in circles around it one moment, side to side the next moment, then up and down sending Maggie into even higher degrees of ecstasy. That feeling had been so long in coming to her that she was not going to be long in releasing. Without a warning, she had begun her first climax and her body had taken control over her mind. At last, in the solitude of the isolated cabin she could scream with joy not suppressed by waking the kids. She could feel the waves of passion drifting back and forth in her mid section. Her grip on Michael's hands clamped down like vices as she felt each marvelous orgasmic contraction. Sounds of overwhelming joy flowed from her lips and her heart could barely keep pace with her excited emotions. Her hips moved rhythmically with the motions of Michael's tongue. Another orgasm followed. Michael was extremely excited at the knowledge that he had created such passion and emotion. As he moved upward, toward Maggie, he was taken into her arms and pulled beside her and smothered with kisses. Tears began to flow from Maggie's dark eyes and her happiness was ever so obvious. Michael simply held her quivering body close and each of them stores this moment to memory.

Maggie was thrilled at Michael's patience, tenderness, and caring. As he held her gently in his arms, she knew he was at her service, wanting only to please her, which he had done so very well just moments ago. Now it was her turn to give back to him the feelings she had wanted to release for such a long time. She had not fully recovered from the tingle of her orgasm. She wanted to be careful not to be overly rough, as at that moment she wanted to become a part of him. She felt like a tiger about to pounce on its prey. With a single quick move, Maggie rolled Michael on his back and was on top of him, her legs straddling his pelvis. Looking into his eyes, she throws her head forward forcing her raven hair to propel itself over his pillow and be gently drug along his body with her downward movements.

Noticing that Michael still had his eyes open, she whispered, "Close those eyes, as it's now my turn. You have no idea how long I have waited and yearned for it to arrive."

To which he replied, " I am afraid to shut my eyes, for I fear you might be gone when they reopen."

"No way for two reasons.... no way I will be gone, and no way you are going to be able to keep them open," she whispered and began to tenderly kiss his cheek, chin, down his neck and on his chest.

As she moved her body down, she began to make each kiss end in an ever so tiny suction to raise the skin on his chest. Also she noticed his erection was never totally gone and was being reactivated with her kisses. As she moved down his body with her straddle, she could feel it press against her backside, leaving drops of moisture in its path. It was a feeling each of them enjoyed. As she continued to move down, just after it rolled across her clit, it sprang forward with the quickness of a trap door.

Maggie had meant to take her time, slowly driving him into a frenzy of desire. That quick motion aroused her and her hand was no longer under her mind's control. She wrapped her fingers around the middle of his shaft and gently squeezed upward. She was keenly aware of the gush of silky clear fluid flowing on her hand. She immediately placed it back on his shaft and began to slowly spread it up and down. Her heart skipped a beat at the groan Michael made. She knew she was doing her job well. This was just the start, she thought, as she positioned herself between his legs. She was now moving in a faster motion and Michael's hand moved from her head to her hands, to slow down the intensity. Thank God, she thought, knowing she was equally caught up in the emotion, and totally stopped her movement while she began to position herself once more.

Once she found herself just over his tense member, she remembered what his breath on her moistened clit had felt like. She slowly began to blow her breath on the moist reddish head. She could almost feel the coldness and excitement with Michael's reaction. His reaction only served to continue to stimulate her. Longing for this moment, the tip of her tongue began to gently glide to the back side of his very hardened instrument. Her frame was so tiny; he picked her body completely up off the bed with his body's reaction. Soon with a combination of both her hands and her mouth, working in perfect unity, she had him so aroused he begged her to stop, to save his unexpected climax. She did and his arms lifted her to his right side. Just then, he sat up and positioned himself again between her legs. Looking once again, she was captured by his blue eyes.

His lips started to speak and he cut himself short, not letting the words come forth. The sun was setting over the western mountains at the lake's edge and the room was very dark. Maggie could barely see as his lips began to move yet they were silent. His arms extended toward her face, his hands once again felt her face, down her neck, and over her shoulders. As he started down her arms, he stopped at the elbows and gently caressed each breast, cupping and uplifting them with his fingers as his thumbs circled the pebble hard nipples. This was all Maggie could stand, and her hands reached down finding his erection, and slowly began to massage her clit. Both of them were lost in the feeling and Michael moved his hands to support his weight. Just then, an extremely odd thing happened. All of a sudden their action and movement stopped. She could have sworn she felt a large drop of warm moisture on her breast. It was almost totally dark in the room, with the exception of one small lamp in the kitchen area, and she could not see Michael's face. Soon she was lost again as the movement of his body against hers began to take control.

With the ease of the combination of each of their lubrications the action quickly became very intense. Her masturbation with his penis in hand had brought her again to begin to feel an eruption coming on. She knew from the animation of Michael's body, that he too was also about to arrive at his time. In less than a second, Maggie had placed his throbbing manhood inside her opening and guided it swiftly into the hot wetness of her lusty tunnel. Almost instinctively Michael makes a quick thrust and Maggie takes in a quick breath from the momentary pain and shock. Her mind easily forgets the pain and is now being taken farther and farther into her fantasy.

As each move becomes quicker and harder, it is just a matter of time until the climax of their passion begins to mix and spills out wet, warm, and wildly on their bodies, as well as everything they touch. Now, totally unable to control their bodies, in the last seconds of lust, they are entwined in each other's passion and explode simultaneously in each other's arms. The movement, although slowed, will continue for several seconds as the extreme tenderness takes hold. Soon their lips meet and they lie tenderly in each other's arms in the afterglow of their pleasure. There was no shame. There was no guilt. There was only peace, joy and satisfaction; it had been much too long overdue.

THE PARTING

It seemed like only minutes had passed as they lay there, without moving, basking in the memories they had just made. The sun had just begun setting long enough to start a chill in the air of the cabin. Maggie must have allowed herself to drift off to sleep for a short time. She noticed the bed was empty and could hear Michael speaking on the phone in the living room. It was some business conversation and it must have been his lawyer because of some of the terms he was using. It did not keep her attention long, and she rose from the bed looking for the most convenient thing to put around her chilling body. There was a multi-colored afghan on a chair beside the bed, just large enough to cover her slender frame. She quickly went to the bathroom to see what a mess she had become and noticed the gleam in her eyes of the left over pleasure Michael had brought to her. Feeling secure, she stepped out of the bedroom, only to find Michael dressed and he appeared to be involved in a deep conversation. He also seemed a bit nervous with Maggie in hearing distance. Soon his conversation was ended. Maggie walked up, opening the afghan wide with both hands, and wrapped her arms around him.

"I can stay if you want another try at total perfection," she said as she began to gently caress his body. Michael bent down to her waiting ear and whispered,

"Are you totally happy? I mean with your life as you have it today? Be perfectly honest with yourself as well as me." Such a question, after such a session startled Maggie and she was taken aback.

"You chose a fine time to ask that one," Maggie said, and released her arms from around him. "You have just given me the most fantastic love making experience of my life, and you want to know if I am totally happy? " I think that answer is clear enough by my overall satisfaction level." Maggie said, her eyes were once again locked to Michael's.

Just then she knew instinctively that if she didn't speak quickly, he would. She was uncomfortable with this situation at the moment.

"Michael, tell me more about yourself, I know hardly anything about you, except I must trust you with my life, alone here with you where no one would know where to locate me," she said as just then the reality of her words clicked in her head. "Your silence only serves to present a mystique about you, and after all..."

He interrupted, "After all, this will never happen again, so why involve yourself to a greater degree with that which will only cause you pain?" Michael paused and the expression on his face changed to a more apologetic one and he continued. "I'm sorry to be so quick, it's not your fault. Everything has been so perfect with you. Sincerely, I could not have found so much pleasure in the wildest most far away places in my imagination." Maggie turns to the bar, asked Michael if he wants another glass of wine, and pours herself another.

In passing, Maggie reaches for Michael on her way to the

couch. She takes his hand and guides him beside her.

"Then what is the matter? Are you having problems at home? At work? Or with me because it would take a blind person not to notice the serious mood," she said in a slow, soft, comforting way.

"Did that phone conversation upset you?" Maggie asked. "I just wanted to know." She repositioned herself and leaned back as though to turn the conversation over to him.

Michael smiled, his eyes began to gleam and almost laughing, he said, "You're damned intuitive. You know that, I guess I knew it from the start as well." Positioning himself closer to Maggie, he began to speak. "My home life is fine. I have a wife who adores me, with the exception that my other love is my work and takes me away from her and our children. The business is now to the point where I am not required to constantly oversee every little detail and can have time off for a change. And having said that, you are probably wondering why I was here with you?"

To which she quickly responded, "Well, yes! now we're talking," she said inquisitively, but was afraid of the response.

"And you are here purely because I wanted you, in more ways than one of course!" he said

"You must also understand that ' wanted you' meant I wanted you, not your body alone. I began to reflect on my life several years ago. As I pondered those things I had longed for and truly wanted. I always achieved them, fully and much more abundantly than expected. I was forced by fate to decide one more wish and you were this desire. I've told you repeatedly, how you were everything I had conceived. That was very true and not a line I was handing you. Every detail about you is exactly what my mind brought to life. You have no way of knowing the importance you have to me, and the very special purpose for which I created your image in my mind. And, that is why I asked you if you were truly happy." Michael said with his same smile and intrusive eyes. "All I want to hear from you is your answer to what do you want?" Maggie was thrown totally off guard at his question, but knew he was very serious.

"Michael, how do you know I want anything?" she asked, knowing he possessed the ability to be extremely capable of knowing her intimate thoughts. With just the one word response, "Maggie..."

She knew it was time to come clean. "Yes, Michael, even in the presence of both my husband and my two children, I AM LONELY, and don't know why," she said in a voice of despair.

"Very well, I have a gift for you..."

"No!" Maggie interrupted, "I can't accept any form of gifts, I would not be able to hide my reactions of memories around my family."

"Not that type of gift Maggie. It is a treasured prize many seek and only a limited few are chosen to find. The path is simple to discover, but laden with self-imposed obstacles. You will receive my gift very soon. I know now that you will know how to put it to your best advantage. Now, I must take you back to Peaches. I have some important things I must tend to tonight," he said, and excused himself from her side.

Maggie didn't know exactly what to feel. She could and

wanted to stay longer, have just one more wonderful experience with Michael, and now wanted to know more about THE GIFT. She also knew it was getting late and her husband might just call for a change, while visiting his brother, and she needed to be home. She took a quick shower and dressed in the bathroom, shy for some reason, and within minutes, was ready to leave. Michael secured the front door, saw Maggie into his car, and in seconds they were leaving that most wonderful memory.

The conversation back to Peaches was extremely limited. Perhaps each was savoring the last few moments together, or maybe preparing for the long silence each was destined to endure. It was evident the moment was quickly ending. Experiencing would have been the wrong word, for they shared those moments. Goodbye was something they each understood was said from the start, yet never wanted to face. To them, there was no tomorrow, no yesterday only today.

The soothing CD played, was inviting, calming, and like most things about Michael, unique in itself. Maggie commented on how fond she was of it. The music seemed to bring a perfect end to the very special occurrence they had just shared in just a moment of time in their existences. His reply was quick, to the point, and unusual.

" Good, this is an opportunity to see just a fraction of the power of THE GIFT. You will be given a cassette of this music to remember me," he said, with that grin to which Maggie had become so attached.

She could almost see the total happiness and contentment he was feeling. Somehow, she knew instinctively how he was feeling. Soon they were parked beside her car at Peaches. As it started at the cabin, a kiss was needed to now end this experience. Unlike the first kiss, this one was passionate in a much different manner. This was a much softer, gentle experiential kiss, more intended to be remembered by each of them. Their tongues lightly touched and savored the minute, the hour and that day. There was still an ember of desire left over, but each one knew they must part, and silence was best.

" I'll be fine Michael, no need for you to walk me to my car," Maggie said, as she opened the door and walked away.

THE ENDING

Maggie's drive home was longer than her original trip to Peaches. She had much to consider and unlike the ending at the cabin, this one was going to take longer and last her a lifetime. As she drove, she thought, How silly, we don't even know each other's last name. As her concentration tried to return to reality, too many questions were upon her mind. Would she ever see Michael again? What was the gift he was sending? Why did she want to complicate her life more with him? Where was her relationship going with her husband? When would these questions be answered? All these thoughts came rushing in at once. She was still affected by the excitement she and Michael had just shared. Perhaps a drink and a whirlpool bath would help bring her thoughts more in order, she thought as she pulled into the drive of her dark, lonely home. She wasn't expecting anyone to be returning until Sunday.

She opened the door, flipped the lights on and went straight to the bedroom to change into something comfortable. Having worn no underwear, she was surprised at herself for enjoying the feeling, then again in her present mood, she could enjoy most anything. Her dark green robe was hanging on the back of the closet door and it felt very comfortable next to her skin. ` Now to get that drink and start to sort out some things.` Upon reaching the bar, and wanting her favorite quick acting alcohol antidote for confusion, she saw a bottle of J&B

Scotch they had gotten for the few and far between drinkers. She remembered Michael again and poured herself a drink. She thought, That was his drink! She pondered all the questions she had thought about on the way home. What if he wanted to meet her again? she wondered. Would she go again? She had desperately needed what she had with him, for such an awfully long time. Her thoughts were extremely pleasant and she wondered about THE GIFT. What was it? How big? What color? 'No it was "a prize" he called it, what kind, of what value... that could wait' she thought, What about her future relationship with her husband? This experience had made her begin to think seriously about her desires, needs and wants. She was not satisfied and had known it for some time.

She felt so alone with all these questions. This was one subject she could not even begin to discuss with any of her closest friends. She had played the game the way everyone might have anticipated, and to reveal she was human would reveal she was a sinner, harlot, loose woman and every other despicable person she felt like at the moment. Relaxed, with the effects of the scotch, which she had rather enjoyed, it was time for a whirlpool bath. She cut off the lights and retired to the master bedroom bath. There she lit many scented candles as the tub was filling. The green robe and her slippers were all she had to remove. Her body slid slowly down the back of the basin and into the hot water. The moment she flipped the switch on, and the jets began to force water in every direction over her body, she began to relax. Her mind drifted back into thoughts again of Michael and what had happened earlier in the day. She scratched an itch on her shoulder and was surprised at how quickly her nipple responded to her arm. Her body was once again in the bed with Michael and ripples of the purest pleasure rolled up and down her like a vibrator. Her hand quickly responded and soon she was satisfied once more with just his memory. She lay there several minutes content in the ecstasy and realized it was time now to sleep.

The next morning Maggie arose much later than usual and was slow to start the day. What the hell? She was alone, her husband and the kids were not due for several hours anyway. What was the big hurry? She took her time, relaxed and enjoyed the solitude. She was glad they had subscribed to the late edition of the Sunday news. She started looking around for something to wear, as she had to go all the way to the street to get the paper. An old tattered raincoat and a pair of worn out running shoes were in the hall closet and just what she needed. Who was going to see her at 10:00 A.M Sunday morning anyway? She dashed out the door, down the drive, quickly retrieved the paper in its plastic bag, and turned to dash for the door. Not in time, Jodi Hiller, the next door neighbor saw her and shouted, "Maggie, Maggie I have something for you, just wait a moment and I'll bring it over," she said as she ran in the house.

Good grief Jodi! Maggie thought, Here I am in this garb and you want me to stand around waiting for someone to see me. Maggie paced impatiently; it was a long established characteristic movement when she was annoyed.

Jodi was a great neighbor and would do anything for her, but the timing was a bit off today. She soon came back out and began to speak,

"Bob and I joined a record club several months ago. As a bonus for ordering additional selections, they sent us this cassette. We already had it given to us last Christmas by our son and his wife. I enjoyed it so much that when this extra came in I immediately thought of you, and now it's yours," Jodi said, taking another breath and preparing to speak again.

Maggie, quickly accepted it saying, "Thanks Jodi, I am sure I will just love it, but I've got to get back inside before someone sees me. You don't mind do you?" and turned toward the front door.

"Oh, no Bob and I were just going to take a trip in the..." Maggie was now almost out of hearing range, "Well, I'll tell her about it when we get back." Jodi stopped and returned to the house.

Maggie looked at the tape and didn't recognize the title or the artist. She just thought it was another something extra to give away and laid it down by the paper on the table and made the coffee. As the coffee was brewing, she remembered she needed to take her birth control pills. She had moved them from the kitchen counter to her purse yesterday. When she opened the purse, to her surprise there was an envelope with her name written in long hand on the outside. She knew it must have been from Michael. She took it and put it next to the cassette Jodi had just given her. The coffee was almost done. She found her favorite cup, filled it and sat down and for a moment, stared at the letter next to the tape. It was now beginning to come to her. She quickly took the cellophane cover off the tape and placed it in the stereo system. It was as Michael had told her "...you will be given a cassette of this music to remember me." She instantly knew. As the sounds began to come forth from the speakers, her thoughts were confirmed. It was the same music as in Michael's car. How could this be happening? How could he have been so sure? What was she going to find next? She carefully opened the envelope containing a letter and another envelope.

With her first sip of coffee she began to read.

"Maggie, it is extremely difficult for me to know where

to begin. There are so many things I wish to reveal to you. I only know that you will be able to totally grasp them all in time. First of all, why did we get together is most likely your first question. Not by accident, I have uncovered a marvelous secret that has come about by years of thought and meditation. One might call it "The Secret of Life", so to speak. If you were not as I thought you would be, you would not be reading this now. I trust I can share it with you for you in turn, you will share it with someone else later. There are two parts to this letter, you are correct in starting with this one first, and afterwards, when you are ready, break the seal on the other and THE GIFT will be revealed to you. Some parts may at first appear confusing and at times very difficult to achieve. They are not and, in a matter of time, you will soon learn to use them for the delivery of your wildest dreams of happiness. They are not important now, you are however, and you deserve an answer to your questions," the note said.

"I chose you because of several reasons for both myself and you. I have long since lost the romance and passion, if I had ever had it, in my marriage. Your physical image as well as your physical desires wanting to be released is what I conceived in my mind. Because using the power does not allow one to be selfish, your needs were also taken into consideration. I have no way of knowing what they may be, but this experience has brought them to your attention. For whatever reason, you were chosen to fulfill my last desire. I can only trust you will recognize it as truth and act wisely upon it. The Gift will see to that.

My life has been a charmed one to say the least. Growing up in a well-to-do family, I had everything I wanted, I thought. As I grew older, I was not satisfied with having everything given to me. I needed something else and went looking for it. I have lived so much of my life searching for this elusive objective. I was aware I must seek from within myself, as you will do, to find that which has been with you all along. All this may seem confusing, but it is not. On the contrary, once you use your own key to unlock the secrets within you, it will become perfectly clear. I found my search had taken me far beyond the limitations of this body, this earth, and even the human existence. Please don't be frightened that you were with a complete lunatic, for what we too often look at as insanity, is indeed the understanding for which we have searched. Although we find the plain teachings of Christ simple and easy on the surface, we make it difficult on ourselves trying to follow them, and create stumbling blocks along our way. You will know, if you do not already, what you must do to find your own happiness. The Gift will help show you how to prepare yourself.

"Once I found a much higher plane of existence, I no longer needed the things I had grown so dependent on as necessary for life. I knew I had outgrown even my own self and would soon have to leave. It was in knowing this thought that in a weakened moment, I allowed my body to take on something even the soul could not interfere. I found out several years ago that I had an inoperable, incurable cancer, which would eventually, with the reality of my blessings, take me from this place. The final stages of this problem would be devastating on my family, as well as the personal burden I would be forced to bear. I was allowed to have a full and final desire, and you Maggie were there. Not of myself alone, for as I hope you will see from hints I will give you, and from the truth which lies inside your own dreams, you are the one to whom I must pass on The Gift, as you will one day pass it to another. For whatever reason we met, we are both blessed. You are now freed to search for and become the person you truly wish to become, whatever this may be. Know that you were loved enough to be created, enough to share, and enough to have The Gift bestowed because you are enough. With my undying love and affectionate wishes, I will always remain with you when needed,

Love Michael Damien "

Maggie was taken back to find that of all the women he could have had, he chose her to share such intimacy. In her mind, she knew she was not in love with him, but also knew she could never forget, his eyes, graying hair, his special smile and laugh. At the same time she began to realize what Michael did mean to her. She desperately sought the attention and ego stroking he provided. Although appreciative, she was not in love with him. With this brutal honesty, she realized she was not in love with her husband either, and she faced what she was in reality for the very first time.... weak. She had spent her entire life striving to please, willing to sacrifice and yielding to other's demands and inside secretly resisting. She never resisted with Michael, and by not resisting him, she allowed the first window to be opened, letting in the pure light so she might see more clearly. She closed her eyes and pictured Michael's face one more time, recalled his caress, his tenderness and his joy. Would she ever see him again? Could they relive that moment of time so precious to each of them? The music was still playing, helping to bring those times back vividly, and Maggie knew she needed to rest her thoughts. What's in the newspaper to take this off my mind? she thought.

As she pulled the paper from the plastic bag, the paper sprang open and, for a second her heart stopped beating. There was Michael's picture on the front page. It was unmistakably him and his smile. Maggie's heart sank again at the headline PROMINENT LOCAL BUSINESSMAN FOUND DEAD OF APPARENT SUICIDE Maggie now knew more than she wanted to know about Michael. Numbed by her present feelings, a single lonely tear fell on his face, as his tear had fallen on her breast. She slowly reached for her coffee cup with a slight tremble, and gazed at THE GIFT.

THE GIFT

Maggie stared at the picture on the front of the late issue of the Sunday morning paper. Stunned and numb from yesterday's encounter with Michael, she could not bring herself to believe in her heart he was now gone. How could that son of a bitch do this to me? she thought and her first and only real emotional movement was her hand crashing down hard on the table. She could not break down. No, she would not break down. She felt betrayed. First Michael had given her a marvelous moment of pleasure and hope, then had taken it away with his own hands. For the strangest reason, she remembered a Bible verse from John 1:1 "In the beginning was the word, and the Word was with God....". This Gift would be his legacy to her, and she had little awareness of the importance it would bring to her life.

It was too late to open THE GIFT. She was not sure how long it would take to read it. Besides, she knew her family would soon be returning home. Usually she was eager to greet them; today she was not. As the cassette continued to play it brought back the words Michael said, even more the ideas he alluded to. His surety of himself in everything he did. She began to feel a change coming about in her mind, yet even more, her soul. For the first time since reading the news of Michael's death, she noticed she was still wearing the raincoat and running shoes. The phone had rung several times, but the sound never reached her ears. She was just now coming back into the real world.

She cursed aloud and vowed that no one would know about Michael or the hurt she was feeling inside. What good would it do anyway? she thought. Who gives a damn? Her normal personality was fighting to regain control, but her loss and bitterness were winning. About this time, she heard her husband's truck pull in the driveway, and she hurried to change clothes and think of an excuse why the house had only gotten messier in a day and a half. She worked better under pressure, and realizing now she had it under control. She came out dressed from the bedroom as the front door was opening.

"Hi Mom, any mail or calls for me?" her son asked, as he streaked by her to his room, never giving her a glance.

Her daughter Nicole did her the courtesy of looking at her when she complained about being trapped with her cousin for a full day. Then said, "Did I have any calls, MOM?" as if Maggie was an answering service.

She replied, "If you did, they're on the answering machine, I was out yesterday, and didn't want to answer the phone today. I have a headache." Her husband came in the door. "What's for dinner Maggie? Gotta put these plans up before I loose 'em!" he said without a kiss, hug, or a how ya doing.

She just stopped and wondered if she was even missed. No need to feel guilty, the only time she would be noticed was if she was not there to be a mother, housekeeper and wife.

Maggie remembered the cassette playing, but not in time. Her husband asked about it, in a sarcastic tone, and Maggie just turned it off saying Jodi had given it to her earlier. Then he noticed the paper, and read the caption about Michael. "Looks like money can make ya crazy... This loser just popped himself for no good reason," he said. Now he... no, all of them, had gone too far with Maggie.

"Can't you guys have the decency to ask how I am, instead of what's in here for you? As for you Roy, I guess you and I will never know if he was crazy or what, will we? I'm going for a jog. You guys can change your attitudes now, or get back in the truck and ride around till you do!" Saying this, it was out the door and down the street for Maggie.

They all looked at each other for a second and blamed the headache. Not much was said later that night, just as Maggie had expected. She only wondered what she would do if Roy wanted to make love. She was in no mood. Maggie just let time take its course, and he went off to sleep as usual.

Next morning Maggie pulled back in her parking space at work, where it all had begun only a few days before. It took an extra effort for her to concentrate and get ready for working. The walk from the car to the elevator was slow. Once there, she saw her friend Pat from another department.

"Oh Maggie, how was your weekend? We just had the most exciting time going to the mountains for a family retreat." Pat said in her usual cheerful way. Maggie would floor her cold as a dead fish if she told her a one liner of her experience with Michael. So she just said, " I was alone most of this weekend. Roy took the kids up to his brothers to visit while he helped him with a project."

Once Maggie got settled at her desk she noticed an uncomfortable quiet in all the rushing around. Something was different this morning. All the partners were in, which in itself was odd, but to be in early on a Monday was exceptional. She wanted to speak with Carl Dunlop about what he had told Michael about her. Likely as not, with all the partners in, this was out of the question. Something was wrong and Maggie wanted to know exactly what. Linda Shannon was Carl's secretary and could give her the low down on what was going on with the big wheels.

Maggie walked over to Linda's desk and quietly asked, "What' are all the partners doing here so early Linda? Is something wrong? This is a Monday you know?"

Linda was too quick to reply, "Oh, just had something come up over the weekend needing everyone's attention."

Maggie knew it was not just a little something. "Linda, this is me, Maggie. I don't have time to play these games this morning. Now what the hell is going on with the company?" Maggie asked giving her the look that got results.

"OK, but you didn't hear it from me, promise Maggie?"

"Yeah, Yeah, what is it?"

"There was another partner, a secret partner you might say. This weekend he killed himself. He had strong financial backing in some of the accounts the company has as better income producers. They're worried and that's all I know, honest. " Linda said with a puzzled look.

'Michael was involved here, too.' Maggie thought. How was she going to talk to Carl now? She just could not admit to having a one-day affair. There was a great deal about Michael that was coming out, and she was not sure she wanted to know more about him.

Maggie went back to her desk and got started on several loose ends, which needed to be tied up. After several cups of coffee and a bran muffin, Maggie was caught up. She walked over to Linda's desk and asked to see Mr. Dunlap.

"Sorry you can't, not for the rest of the day. All the directors are going to the funeral, then meeting with clients afterwards. Sorry." Linda said.

For a moment Maggie felt the guilt pour over her like honey. Here she had enjoyed a once in a lifetime experience with a man she didn't know and felt guilty about not going to his funeral. There was no love there, or was it hidden in some remote part of her heart? It was not fair, she thought. Not fair at all to wait a lifetime to derive joy from a moment's pleasure, purely because she had allowed her heart to want selfishly for a change. All those thoughts suddenly brought the possibility of tears to her eyes. Thinking she was far too strong for that type of emotion, besides the rest of the office would wonder why. She began to think of what she would do to disguise those feelings from herself. Later that day, when it was almost dark, after any possibility of anyone being there, she went to the cemetery and among all the many flowers she gently laid down a single white rose. How strange how it appeared to be the only one present. A single tear rose from her heart,slowly made its way down her cheek , she turned and walked away.

The next day Maggie saw her opportunity to take off and read THE GIFT. The weather was perfect. She could go home, change, pick up some fruit for lunch, and read in the park. She could not go to Michael's service alone, though she wanted to very much. She remembered the conversation was short going back to Peaches. Her heart fell again remembering she had not given him time to say goodbye, now she was unable to say it to him.

In the park was a huge oak tree, with long extending branches. Somehow, a tree of its gigantic size seemed to absorb and nurture those who longed to find solace from a lonely heart. It was Maggie's favorite place to just sit and think, or it used to be. It had been a very long time since she had even had the opportunity to take a moment off and spend time alone with just herself and her thoughts. Because it was Tuesday, the squirrels were out running, but the people weren't. The birds were busy singing. The smell of newly mowed grass filled the air. It was a great time to open and enjoy the last words from Michael.

She re-read the first letter and noticed it was typed out, but THE GIFT was in an envelope with the title on the outside of a plain white envelope written in longhand. She held them tightly and made herself comfortable, opened the envelope and took out its contents. There was a single sheet letter wrapped on the outside of several pages. Maggie began to read:

"Maggie, this is an addition to this gift I wanted to put in just for you. I had no doubts that you would receive it, and I wanted to express my own personal thanks and thoughts. You will first notice the pages of THE GIFT are much older. There is a reason for this. TIME. This is perhaps the hardest true conception you will have to learn. As humans, we are all very guilty of impatience and want to rush time, as if we could. I have had THE GIFT for over twenty-five years. There is no telling who or how long someone else may have had it. You will notice the almost broken creases in the folds, the yellowing of the paper, and the faded ink of the pen. I have read it many times, as you will do. It is only through your repeated reading that understanding will come about. It is the quiet time afterward which the voice inside you will reveal that which you wish to know. You are indeed very special. It took two years to concentrate on your every feature before I was allowed the honor and the privilege of meeting you and having my last wish FULFILLED. You will understand more as your journey continues. I am writing this down in the hope of saving you time by doing things in a much more beneficial manner.

First, after you have read the entire contents of THE GIFT, you will want to secure the best paper you can find and the best writing instrument also. After all, you will be referring to these pages for a long time to come until you have mastered it's contents, and are ready to give it to the next person designated later to you, as its recipient. This is going to be the best change your life has ever seen, and will continue to get better from this moment. Please write in longhand the entire contents of the pages that follow.

Now, this is important, and may at first be very difficult for you to follow. After you have made one, and only one, copy of THE GIFT in your own handwriting, you are to destroy this copy by burning until it remains only ashes. There are several reasons for this act. One, you will better put my memory to rest, and two you will have a new start with your own copy in which you personally wrote each and every word down. This is all I can allow. Believe me when I say our relationship will again one day be restored, if this is your wish. From now on, your wishes will come true, but only if you truly know they will.

Michael

Maggie paused for a moment thinking of every second she had spent with Michael. She repositioned herself next to the tree, and opened the first page of THE GIFT and began to read. For a minute or two, she never read a word, only noticed his longhand. It was very neatly written and, reflecting good penmanship, every letter was the same height and in perfect line. She paused to think if this was a reflection on his character. He had seemed that way from the very beginning to her. Somehow, she could not picture any less of him, remembering the perfect way the knot was formed in his tie. She laughed as that thought passed through her mind. There was so much to recall, yet it was the little things she found so unforgettable. It was like being with him all over again as she let her eyes focus on the lines rather than the words. There before her in blue ink on faded white paper was Michael. Could she burn it? she thought. It would be most difficult for if the wind did not blow out the match, her shaking hand would surly extinguish the flame. She paused a while from simply looking at his words and wondered if there was really ever a flame between them. She knew the depth of the physical union, but could only wonder if he was more than simply a long hidden desire. He was gone now, and she had to deal with what he had left behind. She opened THE GIFT and it simply read:

You have been selected to receive this Gift for several reasons. One, the person presenting it to you has been lead to the knowledge that you should have it, and two, you have requested assistance with a particular situation in your life. There are several things you must do in order to begin to benefit from these simple truths. As soon as possible, you are to obtain the most durable paper you can find, copy the entire contents of this document, word for word, and destroy this original. You must also never reveal this to anyone. There is only one requirement, that you have faith or that you allow your faith to grow, to believe in what is contained here. You already possess everything needed to utilize this Gift. You must only read the following words until your faith is secure in yourself and you are prepared to receive those things you truly want.

If you do not go within, you will go without!

From within you know you are already there!

There are only two rules:

You have the power to be, do, and have whatever you can imagine.

You attract that which you most fear and reject the real possibilities because of the experiences of others, not your own. Open up to your own thoughts, feelings, emotions and experience your own potential.

You are made up of the Soul, the Mind, and the Body for good reason. Whatever the soul can conceive, the mind can create for the body to experience. Every human has this ability to every degree.

There are no limitations on you and consequences of each request will be based on whether or not you included the following elements in the desires of your heart.

1. Accepting 2. Blessing 3. Gratitude 4. Joyfulness 5. Loving

You will know you have achieved your highest idea when these are revealed and realized in your desires.

In order to go within your true self, picture a lake in your mind. When all the ripples are gone and the surface is calm and still, look deeply into the water. The voice inside will guide you from there. Your desires are only waiting for the power of your thoughts, words and actions to be realized.

That's it? She thought. Maggie sat back against the tree and wondered what this was all about. Could this have really been from Michael? What was it she was to see? How was she to go and find that which were her highest ideals? First things first, she thought, she needed to drop off some laundry today, first thing. The day was a total waste and she would not go back to the office.

As Maggie came out of the dry cleaners she noticed a shop across the street simply titled "Antique Books". Upon entering the door, the musty smell of leather, paper and dust affected her breathing and she sneezed softly.

"Sorry for the smell," a voice called from the back, "Some of these books have been with me for years."

A most delightful old man came around an aisle of books.

"Good afternoon, my name is Joseph. I am the proprietor of this non-profit business. It was not designed to be non-profit originally, as that was not my true intention," he said laughing as he took off his apron.

Maggie smiled at the comment and asked, " How long have you been here? I've been coming to the dry cleaners across the street for years and this is the first time I have noticed your store."

"You just must have been in a rush, you can tell by the smell alone, we have been at your service for a while," Joseph claimed. He was a short man, mid sixties, with snow white hair, bright blue eyes and a laugh that would comfort most anyone. She felt very easy around him as if he were a grandfather or an uncle.

"Oh, I was looking at a very old letter today and my mind was into antiques, and you look like you have enough around to suit most anyone's purpose," Maggie said, starting to pick up things from a table.

"Yes, yes, we have almost anything you may need regarding writing, even the writing itself. One time, I had an old gentleman come in who wanted a post card. We found one and he asked if I would mind addressing it for him. It was no problem for me, so I did. He explained he was a bit shaky and asked would I fill in a line or two, which I also did. After that, he wrote on the bottom, 'forgive the messy handwriting'."

Maggie found the tale most amusing and felt even more at ease. " Well, I just wanted to locate some durable writing paper for a very special purpose. Do you carry anything like that?" she asked.

"Yes, I have some." answered Joseph, "Be right back." In no time he was back with two sheets of very old paper that he placed on the counter. "This is very special paper. Don't have much request for it any more. Costs too much and these are the very last sheets."

"What makes them so special?" Maggie asked trying to be polite.

A gleam came into Joseph's eye and a smile on his face as he said, " They're magic. You're welcome to 'em. No one wants magic paper anymore these days. People just don't believe in magic," he smiled and winked.

"Well," Maggie said with the first smile she had worn that day. "In that case, how much are they? I can always use some magic paper."

Joseph looked at her, this time with a much more serious gaze, and said, "You are welcome to have them, I know you will put them to good use." She was taken back by the tone of his voice and suddenly realized he thought they were really magic.

"Well, I can't just take them for free. You are in business to make a profit, remember? I will need a good pen to compliment the paper. Do you have any of those?"

"Oh, yes, but I'm all out of magic ones today, but any good quality ink will work on that paper." He reached under the counter for an old fashioned fountain pen and a dusty bottle of ink.

The sincerity of Joseph made Maggie humble herself. She felt very much at peace after the ordeal of the last several hours, and his mannerism made her just want to relax.

"You say the paper is magic, Joseph. What makes them magic?" she asked.

"Why you do! Magic is only true in the eye of the magician and the believers who want to see it." he said softly. "That will be $17.77 total with tax," he said and handed her the pen and papers in a previously used bag. She gave him a twenty dollar bill, got the change, and walked away. No other words were exchanged. Maggie got in her car and left to go back home. She thought about how strange it was that she had not noticed the store before, and how much help he was, just when she needed it most.

As she sat at the dining room table, ready to start to re-write THE GIFT on her "magic" paper, she wondered if this was all a game. For that matter, was anything real? The last few days had slapped her in and out of reality too often and too quickly. It was now up to her to take what had happened and either act upon it or forget it entirely. She decided to start to copy the words from THE GIFT down anyway. Her decision to act on it could change at anytime. Her mind needed to be occupied for the moment. As she wrote, the pen seemed to flow much easier than it had ever before. Like a sponge, she was absorbing every word to memory. A very strange sensation washed over her. While she was copying those words down, other words kept coming into her head clearly. For the first time, she could see a precise picture of what she wanted out of life, something she had never been able to conceptual-ize. The emotional experiences were those of joy and sad-ness, relief and sorrow, death and a new life process begin-ning. As she finished the last of the work, an almost uncanny feeling of peace came over her. She smiled and thought where she would start. There was no doubt she would succeed with whatever life might throw her way.

Just as she was finishing up the last of the copying, the phone rang. It was Linda from the office.

"Maggie, where have you been?" she asked in an almost panicked voice.

"I decided to take the rest of the day off, I have enough comp time coming to me. Is there anything wrong?" Maggie asked with a bit of concern in her voice.

"Well, the owners are in a meeting now, have been since their return today, and they have been asking about you. What do I tell them?" Maggie just laughed at the thoughts of how often they always needed her in emergencies.

"Tell them I'll be in tomorrow. Do you know what it's about?" Linda worked well under pressure most times, but she was very uneasy about whatever was going on with the partners this time.

"Maggie, there seems to have been a real crisis at the top. All I know is everyone is very concerned and you are involved somehow. Just be sure to be here in the morning, bright and early, I'll cover for now. Got to go, bye." Silence was left to start Maggie's imagination.

She knew her position was secure. She was a first rate dedicated employee. But what did they want with her? Was Michael involved? she wondered. She refolded THE GIFT with the copies and put them away, work needed her attention at the moment.

The next morning Maggie arrived early, looking her very best, trying to give a confident impression. She was ready for anything, she thought. The partners' cars were all there and whatever it was, to have them all at the office before eight, had to be a major crisis. Everything seemed normal. Linda was at her desk, as usual; the coffee was made, filling the room with its usual strong aroma.

Maggie's desk was filled with the standard pile of notes of calls, denials, and requests. At the top was a note, "Meeting at 9 AM SHARP THE LOUNGE!" The lounge was the grand meeting room where only the partners, the cleaning crew and a few selected others were allowed to enter. It got the name because it was used primarily after hours to entertain clients. There was a rumor alcohol was served there. The lounge was a subject no one discussed.

She finished her coffee, then went to the ladies room and freshened up. At exactly nine she knocked on THE LOUNGE door. Several voices greeted her to come in. They sounded anxious. "Good morning, gentlemen," she spoke quickly and was guided to her awaiting chair positioned at the end of the table. "What is on the agenda this morning?" Maggie asked with a half smile and waited for the first sign of a problem in the office, a compliment about her work. It was not long in coming.

"Maggie, ... may we address you as Maggie?" Carl Dunlap asked and promptly continued without a reply. She simply nodded her head with approval. "We have been extremely impressed with your work in the firm. During the time you have been here..." There was the compliment. Now what's next? Maggie blocked out most of the actual words he was saying as she reviewed the faces in the room. Something, or someone, had a hold on them. They had to make a decision their expressions revealed they preferred not to make. She knew what she had done for the firm and how much money she had brought in, but what was this all about? Why? She had all but given up on the idea of management, when she snapped back to reality as Carl said "...executive manager of a special account, not generally made public." Wait just a damned minute! This is just too convenient Maggie thought. Never had he said anything about it before, not a hint, NOW they're suggesting me? She pondered, and waited to let Carl put it all on the line.

"Of course it would mean a transfer to their location in Arkansas, an office in their poultry plant, and the salary would remain the same. Bonuses would be based on the overall increase in profits," Carl smiled. Like the dog's wagging head in the back of bouncing cars with the crazy shocks, the rest of the partners nodded respectively.

"We know this is all so very sudden, and if you wish to consider the proposal we will understand. Your husband's position and family might present a problem. "

Carl continued to talk as Maggie began to realize what was going on. Michael must have had something to do with whatever this was about, and she was now going to get into the game as a player. Carl's tone changed in an about face manner.

"We understand you might prefer not to take this position. If other family matters present a problem, we are prepared to offer you exclusive management over several other current house accounts. We want to advise you of the actions we are considering and allow you the opportunity to know what your future plans with the firm might be. Do you have any particular questions at this time, Maggie?" Carl closed as he began to recline in his chair. She sensed she was quickly being taken for a ride. Now, if ever, was the time for quick thinking. Her position, the one she had long wanted, was at jeopardy and they thought she had just fallen off the proverbial turnip truck. Whatever she was to say next had to be organized, carefully thought out and forthcoming. She was playing with the big boys now, yet she maintained her calm and prepared to answer.

Maggie placed her hand over her mouth, as she signaled she was considering something. She took a few seconds, pushed herself away from the end of the table.

"I am sure there will be several questions regarding the intricate details of this matter which will need to be discussed at length. However, due to the untimely manner in which I was informed regarding this meeting, I do not have the time to deliberate and must leave for a previous appointment with my attorney." Maggie said as she rose from her chair. Her knees began to question their ability to support her weight as she stated,

"I am not sure what documents you have from Michael Damien regarding this decision. I have not completely finished my review of the ones he gave me. When we have thoroughly digested the information, I shall request a convenient time to reconvene this meeting," she said with the most confidence she had felt in years. She had not only let them know, in a small way, that she had some form of relationship with Michael Damien, but that it was she who had now taken control.

There was an immediate change in the room with the last sound of Maggie's voice. As she turned to leave she recognized the sound of breaths being taken in, and chairs coming away from the table for the partners to stand, something they had failed to do when she came into the room earlier. Walking out the door, she felt how she had wanted to feel for a long time. She closed the door behind her and leaned against it. She could hardly believe what had just happened.

Maggie walked over to Linda's desk, and whispered to her, "I'll be out the rest of the day." Then walked out the door, not knowing what her next move was going to be. She was a total bundle of mixed emotions. Part of her was sad, while another part was joyous. She felt an energy that was available for the first time in her life, yet helpless, not knowing how to tap into the source. All these feelings had started to come about since she read THE GIFT, and if it was to continue, for some reason unknown to her, the answers were locked away in there. She had finished copying the words and she needed to burn Michael's copy. Could she do it? she thought to herself as she drove out of the parking lot. This was the only thing Michael had given her and his last request was to destroy it, but he had said nothing about his accompanying letter, and this thought alone provided the strength she needed at the moment. A quick stop by the house to change clothes, pick up THE GIFT and a book of matches was all she needed.

She felt as though she would physically feel better if she jogged around the park. Once again under the tree in the picnic area, Maggie read THE GIFT in Michael's longhand, walked over to a public grill and hastily set it ablaze, lingering would only stress her courage. For a moment her eyes were fixed on the orange and yellow flames, then it was over. Even the smoke was quickly gone in the breeze and left only the black and gray ashes. If you don't go within, you will go without, kept haunting her. She had never mastered the ability to meditate and didn't want to consider it now. With a sharp turn, she leaped and was running toward the sporting fields.

Running always allowed her to think. Alone as she could be, each thought came to mind clearly, addressed and sorted as if done by a computer. She had been running for at least an hour, when she considered her thoughts. Her heart was pounding from the jog and thinking her strengths had returned she rounded the corner of the park, next to the front entrance. There it was, a long gray car. She was not going to break down. In spite of the aching in her heart, she ran faster. She was not going to cry, she thought, as the tears began forming in her eyes.

The day was warm, the lunch crowd had come and gone, and she was quickly approaching the huge fountain by the entrance. It was a very large one with several tiers. Each layer caused the sound of the water splashing into the bowl to become unbearable. God only knew how she was hurting. With a single leap, Maggie jumped inside the main basin of the fountain. The rush of water pouring over her washed down her uncontrollable tears. The terrible emptiness of her silent cries only brought her loss to a greater degree of misery inside her heart. The sickening feeling left her much more than merely alone. Nothing at the moment could have removed the nauseous sadness. For a minute, she wanted to curse God for the terrible trick he was playing with her life. There was another surge of pain inside her heart and she could not hold back the agony in her voice. Quickly, as the uncontrollable mournful sounds came forth, she looked around. The reality of the moment only added to her despair. There was not even a squirrel to share her sadness. She just stood there alone as the water poured over her raven black, almost waist length, hair. Alone she cried. The spandex outfit seemed to shed the water like a bird's feathers. She felt the coolness and walked out from under the water's flow and sat on the large rim of the fountain's pool. Her head was now in her hands as she started to regain her composure. From nowhere, she felt the warmth of the sweater on her shoulders.

"You looked as if ya might be a wee tad cold, my dear," the man's voice said, just above a whisper.

Maggie had been in her own world so long that the very presence of anyone else totally startled her.

"My God, don't come up behind me and scare the shit out of me like that. Don't you?" Maggie's voice stopped short of finishing her sentence as she turned around finding the voice to be that of a Catholic priest.

"I'm very sorry to have given ya such a fright. You looked not only like a drowned puppy, but also like you had lost your best friend. My name is Shawn O'Hara," he said, placing his hand out to shake, " And you are?"

"Margaret Hobbs, but please, call me Maggie, Father, and sorry for my language," Maggie said smiling. "Here's my hand. My foot is already in my mouth."

"Why that's an odd name... Maggie Father. They used to call me Father Shawn, but it began to make me feel old, so they just call me Shawn now." And they both started to laugh.

"I'm so sorry to intrude on your privacy. You did not notice me before, and I overheard your sorrow. I am in the listening business if you have a mind to talk," he said as his smile began to warm her spirit.

"No I don't think so. I'm not Catholic and I wouldn't know just where to begin if I were, " Maggie replied.

"I'd be out of a job if Catholics were all I talked to. As a matter of fact, I am out of a job right now. I'm just filling in at St. Thomas' Church until a new priest can be found. So ya see, I do have time, " he said as he sat down next to her.

"Well," Maggie said, " you could help me find out how to go within myself. I need to do that and I don't really know how to start. Father Shawn, can you help me with this one?" she said almost in a plea.

"Man, you first say you don't think you want to talk, then you ask the most complicated question in the world. I can only try, but please let's be a bit more informal, call me Shawn, please," he said. " Can we walk as we talk?" They began to walk back toward the playing fields again.

Shawn began to relax Maggie, by talking about some of

the places he had been assigned. From his warm smile, beaming from his lips, to the animation of his body movements, he presented the essence of peace. Maggie found herself drawn in by his low soft voice. There was something about this man that she accepted his knowledge on pure faith. Being middle aged, he could relate to Maggie and helped calm her fears, knowing what indescribable pain he had just witnessed a short while back.

"First of all, one of the reasons I want you to call me Shawn is being a priest puts me at a disadvantage off the bat. Everyone thinks of us as hearing a confession or the lowly father walking behind the condemned prisoner. We're humans and people first, " he laughingly stated. " Have you tried meditation, yoga, and the likes to go within, or would you just like my own personal opinions on the subject? I do have my own opinion in spite of contrary views, " he chuckled, and she affirmatively nodded. Father Shawn continued.

"In order to go within, you must have a good idea of what you are looking for once you get there. I think that as much as God created us in HIS, pardon the sexist thing, image, he or she must reside there in part. We, as humans, have long sought God by way of some great mystical power, which we have made extremely complicated. I don't believe God ever meant anything to be so complicated and hoped every person on earth could understand what he was trying to say. Because we are Christian, and believe in the principles of Christ, I can only speak of those areas, and even then some within my own religion are going to disagree. His story, when we take it just from His words alone is very simple, uncomplicated, and easy to understand. We are guilty of complicating it beyond understanding.

"If you will simply look at only the words of Jesus, not

the deeds written about Him, you can see He is giving a very clear path to finding a way to go within yourself. Once this is accomplished, and you are within, you find God, Once you find God, you have thus ended the search, for you now dwell in pure love, which is our concept of God. Look for a moment at what Jesus tells us. His only two commandments were to love God and to love your neighbor as yourself. Getting there is where we have the problem. Jesus also told us the answer. Faith! We don't HAVE because we don't have the faith necessary to know it is there all the time waiting on us. This, more than anything else, He tells us repeatedly. God is there to give us what we ask. We are here to ask. This is not complicated, but we make it that way because we lack the faith to simply believe. People want to make difficult Grace and Faith, both of which are FREE. All we need is to request, simply, openly and honestly.

"Everything we need has already been provided and is only waiting for our request. We don't truly believe it and therefore it remains always out of our reach. The secret is knowing that everything, no matter what is asked, will be given in the best time for our best interest. We are also guilty of being impatient. Am I making any sense or only confusing you more?" he asked with a warm smile.

"I'm not sure. However, it seems to be getting clearer. Let me repeat what I thought you told me. If I am on the wrong track, you correct me," Maggie said with a growing gleam in her eye. "God, as we understand the being, created us to give us what we ask for, and we are simply here to request anything we want and we must just be patient till it comes! Why, that sounds too simple to believe," she inquiringly said.

Shawn continued to explain. " You see, the first assumption you just made is that it can't be, simply because you can't explain it. Remember it is not something that is going to happen over night. The Bible leaves a gap in the life of Jesus from twelve to thirty-three years of age. What do you think he was doing during those twenty-one years? He was preparing himself to overcome the natural inclinations of a human, that being, doubt and fear, to which we have an abundance. Consider this, Saul, who later became Paul, had to leave for a three year period before he began his ministry. Why? Could it be he needed time to change the way of thinking he had become so accustomed to as a human? " Shawn said and could see the lights begin to come on in Maggie's mind.

"God, that's so simple. I am beginning to see," Maggie stated with the formation of a smile.

"Exactly," Shawn came back. "Your statement could never be any truer, GOD, you made it simple, and you used the powerful statement God gave to Moses, I AM. You are on your way to that which you are seeking. Ask, request, and accept the ability to go within and it will be given. It is all just a matter of how much you believe, and the degree to which you are willing to delve to be able to make the proper request." His voice had a tone signaling the conversation had ended.

"Oh, Shawn I want to talk and visit with you again. I have so many questions and you are so easy to talk to. Please don't leave me as my journey begins," Maggie said as she grabbed his hand.

To which he placed his hand over hers and looking deeply into her eyes said, " You have never been, nor will you ever be left alone, believe me. You found me, for you asked, even if you were unaware and you will never be forsaken. Now, we must get back to our lives. This has been a great visit.

Thank you for allowing me to share these moments and remember, first your thoughts, then your words, then your actions, and you will receive," he smiled, turned and quickly walked away.

Maggie felt as if she had been given a secret to a new beginning. She turned and began to jog back to her car. As she began to drive, her mind began to open up to the thoughts to which she had just been exposed. If it were true that our purpose here was to make requests of God and God's purpose was to grant them, there should not be a limitation to them. Maggie began for the first time to take steps much bolder than she had ever done. The first thing coming to her mind was the "special account not generally made public" was about to be handed over to her for whatever reason. Carl Dunlap had given her a taste and then told her it might make her sick if she swallowed. Maggie thought to herself, If I get this offer, no WHEN I get it, first thing I am going to get is a salary like the others. The men that is. There has never been a woman in management to begin with and I'm going to set the example. The more she began to think about the situation, the more verbal and excited she became. "Wait a minute, I'm not going to have an office in a poultry plant. They can shove that idea up the keester, Mac!" Having assured herself, she began to say out loud what she did want. What would be fair? What would a man expect? $50,000 per year and profit increase incentive bonus. An office outside the plant with my choice of locations. My own private secretary - assistant and a company car. That ought to do it for now." she said smiling and pleased with herself. Then all of a sudden, she began to think of the family. What would Roy think? And the kids... they were about to graduate from high school, she thought. "Oh great, let me have the opportunity of my life and ...NO, I AM NOT LETTING NEGATIVE THOUGHTS IN MY THINKING, not this time. I AM worth something. Roy and I will just have to talk it over. I want this opportunity more than I have ever wanted anything else before, except Michael, and I am willing to fight for it. She pulled into her drive just before the kids were due home from school, and for the first time noticed she still had on Father Shawn's sweater. Her mouth dropped with a surprised look and she wondered why he had not mentioned it. She remembered, he said he was filling in at St. Thomas' Church. She would drop by and give it back as soon as she had a free minute. Right now, free time was not on her agenda. She decided to surprise the family with supper, remembering she had taken off early.

She picked up the Monday paper and went inside the house. The light from the answering machine was blinking and she almost didn't know what to do. The light was new to her; everyone else had always beaten her to it. She managed to quickly figure the system out and got the message. It was Linda from the office.

"Maggie, I don't know what you did to the partners, but they seem to have their hats in their hands when it comes to you. They advised me to call you and let you know it was expected you would take a couple of days off and to call them at your convenience to arrange another meeting." Linda's voice said in a business tone. Then came a quick whisper, "Way to go, girlfriend!" and the call ended.

Maggie couldn't help but smile at what she had accomplished as she started to clean up some of the mess around the house before starting dinner. As she picked up the paper, the obituary section fell out and she could not help reading 'Joseph Michael Damien laid to rest...' she quickly stopped her reading, separated the page, folded it and put it away in a safe place as if to tuck away and save an article precious to the heart, the type that is kept for future inspiration. She slowly moved toward the kitchen to start dinner. The thought whispered through her mind Michael's memory would always remain with her forever, as she felt his presence at every obstacle along her way to growth.

Maggie enjoyed several days off from the office and called to arrange the meeting with the partners on Friday. She had told Roy about the proposals the partners had made, but not knowing all the details at hand, she just decided to discuss it over the weekend when things were more finalized. She had managed to talk to an attorney friend of hers and was advised to wait to see what the partners were going to offer before spending money blindly, but spend money was something Maggie was going to do. She had decided to buy the best looking business suit she could find for the Friday meeting. She would get the things she wanted and was going to look the part to accept their offer. She had arranged the time at 9:00 a.m. sharp and had prepared herself accordingly.

She did not go into the office early; rather she arrived just at the needed moment to knock on the Lounge door at nine. This time there was a much different greeting from the other side. As she walked into the room, the partners rose from their chairs, it was obvious there had been a metamorphosis in their attitude.

Maggie was first to speak. "Good morning, Gentlemen," she said with a quick smile and she sat down at the chair she had left only days earlier.

"I hope you have the complete details and the conditions of the offer we had previously discussed." Those would be her last words for awhile.

To her utter surprise, they began to confess things she

could never have imagined, and as she thought, Michael did have an interest in the firm and the account. It seems he held a sufficient amount of stock in the client's company to dictate conditions. The whys and wherefores of his ability were not important to Maggie, but it was extremely obvious Michael's power was there. The partners handed her the multi-typed pages of her contract, and as she quickly reviewed its contents. Maggie felt an extreme urgency to excuse herself to get to the ladies room, but remained calm and collected. There it was in front of her in black and white. She was going to get a salary of $50,000 per year, a very nice percentage of profit incentive bonuses, an office with her choice of location, and an assistant-secretary. She scanned a bit faster and found it. Yep there it was; a company car. All of a sudden she experienced this compelling feeling to shout, but kept her composure to smile very politely and excused herself with the promise after she reviewed the full contents of the offer, an answer would be forthcoming Monday morning. With that, the partners again rose from their chairs as Maggie exited the room.

Maggie winked at Linda as she left, this time not even stopping to say where she was going. There was much to do. Her excitement level was up. Now it was time to prepare herself and family for what was going to take place next. What am I going to do? What is Roy going to do? she thought as she left the building. Suddenly, she began to realize what she had said she wanted had come about. Without question, it was there in black and white in the proposal. She smiled with joy at the thoughts of things to come. She knew THE GIFT had caused significant changes in her life in a very brief time. Now, to be brutally honest and acknowledge the areas she wanted to change in her personal life. Her marriage was a top priority, and with this new promotion, it was going to be difficult at best. It did not take her long to decide to return to the park with THE GIFT and a pen and pad to outline things she was going to see changed. For some strange reason, her attitude toward everything had taken on a new outlook, much more positive than before. For the first time in her life she saw herself as a person who was in charge of her own emotions, desires, and conceptualized ideas of what she wanted, rather than what she thought someone else might want. With a quick trip by the house she was soon dressed in her running outfit and jogging on the path at the park. Each time she read THE GIFT it seemed to speak to her with more clarity and focus on the areas she needed to address in order to accomplish her task at hand. She realized it was not only her right, but more her obligation to herself, to bring about the changes in her life that would not only benefit her, but everyone around her as well. In the last few days, she had unconsciously found herself walking differently, the animation of her body was new and she was much happier. Just now, realizing the new found power she had uncovered within herself, she could not help but smile.

Time seemed to slip away, and she needed to do several things before going home to start dinner. She stopped by the dry cleaners to pick up the clothes she had left days before and decided to return to the book store and visit with the old man who had been so courteous. They had changed the storefront since she had been there. Upon entering, the past musty odor of books was gone and the counters and shelves were totally arranged in another order. A lady was reading at the cash register, and casually looked up over her glasses and as if it were an imposition, she quickly asked,

"Help ya ma'am?"

"No thank you I just was going to say hello to Joseph, is he in today? " Maggie asked.

"Joseph who, ma'am?" the woman asked putting her book on the counter.

"Joseph, the owner of this store. I purchased some paper from him a few days ago. He didn't tell me his last name."

"There is no one by that name here. The owner of the store is Mrs. Lowman. I'm sorry," the clerk said with a puzzled look on her face.

"Well the place looks altogether different. Has it just been purchased? I know I spoke with Joseph here last week. I even purchased some paper and a pen." Maggie was now becoming a bit aggravated.

"I'm sorry again. We do not sell paper or pens. Could it have been another store?"

"It was this store and the man who waited on me was named Joseph," Maggie said as she turned and exited the door. What in the world is going on? I know what I know! she thought. She was getting in the car when she noticed Father Shawn's sweater, in the back seat. Well, I can take this back to St. Thomas' Church. I know I talked to Father Shawn, she thought. Upon arriving at the church Maggie found Father Shawn sitting on a bench outside the church.

"Oh Father Shawn, I'm so glad to see you. For a moment I thought I was losing my mind," Maggie said in a desperate tone.

"It's just Shawn, remember, and I knew you would come back. There are now even more questions in your mind. I just had a feeling you would be back. Now, what is it troubling you Maggie?" he said softly in a tone which compelled her to ask a question she had not known she needed to find the answer.

"Well, there is a question, and I'm not sure how you knew I needed some answers, but I'm just as happy you asked," she said wondering how she would find out details of THE GIFT without disclosing its' presents at the same time. "I have decided to change my life. In these changes I want to always bring forth attributes I feel are most important to me as I change. I just don't know how to apply them in every situation."

"And they are?" he questioned.

"Well, it may sound a bit unusual, but I want each decision to include five elements: Accepting, Blessing, Gratitude, Joyfulness and of course Loving," she figured that was all she needed to say and simply waited for his next words.

"It's good you have chosen those five, they are the cornerstone to understand who you are and how to react to every situation life will place upon you. It is not the easiest course to follow, and over time and with awkwardness at first, you will learn to apply each in the order of importance to every given situation in your life. Acceptance is by far the most important of them all. If you have truly accepted your life has purpose and you design that purpose, you have accomplished the hardest part. Your acceptance of yourself, as you honestly are, is the only way to accept others. You will soon see problems which come your way from the eyes of the others in which you see the problems, or a better word would be situations, are coming from. Acceptance is also the hardest of all the attributes you described. For as humans, we are not of a naturally accepting nature, but that must come in time. Then and only then are you able to bring Blessing into the picture.

Each encounter, event or obstacle in one's life is truly a blessing. It was given to assist in the purpose that you have chosen, and must be seen by you in its reality, a blessing. If you can but greet conditions in your life, pleasant or unpleasant as ALL being blessings, then you will see much more clearly how to absorb and react to them. Once you have mastered the knowledge that all things are given as blessings, in whatever form, then you must acknowledge them with the next element you have mentioned, Gratitude.

"Our hearts never lie to us, regardless of how hard we may try to deceive ourselves. If you are truly to observe conditions which come your way with the attitude of them being a blessing, you must in truth be in a mood of gratitude for what has been sent. This is more or less fortitude of your acceptance of everything being a blessing. Remember I told you, God's job was to grant what you asked, and your job was to ask? Well, would you ask for anything that you were not grateful? One must only have faith in order to accomplish the greater goals of their desires, one must overcome the smaller goals along the way, for those one must be equally grateful. It is when all those things are brought together that you have found and are ready for the last, loving.

"You see, the other components are all in the make up of love. One can not richly practice each aspect without truly feeling the abundance of love, for love is the end result of the joining of those attributes. Love is not something that is felt, for the definition is greatly varying to each individual; however, love is the result of all the positive attempts one makes to guide their life toward the established goal. Once the goal is clear, the heart is sure, the commitment made, there is no way love can be avoided. After all, it is the ultimate of God's wish for you. That is the part of the image of God that was given and that is the part you will ultimately find," he said turning as if he were leaving.

Maggie was awe struck. Never had she heard words so clearly. She had asked, and her request had been answered. Too simple, she thought, but her path was just beginning to be revealed. She was not surprised that it was time for him to leave. She was again at peace. So much so she almost forgot why she came to see him in the first place. When she looked up he was gone. She rushed to the car retrieved the sweater and went inside the church sanctuary. To her surprise, she did not find Father Shawn inside, but a much younger priest attending to his chores.

When she asked for Father Shawn O'Hara, she was told no such person was there. The priest had been there for fifteen years and knew no priest by that name. Maggie was totally beside herself. She knew what had happened with both Joseph and Shawn, and knew equally well that she was not going crazy. As she carried the sweater back to the car, she noticed the tag with the initials JMD and dropped to a bench at the garden on the church grounds.

"Wait!" she said aloud. Shawn O'Hara couldn't be JMD. Then she remembered the obituary in the paper, Joseph Michael Damien.... and for a moment felt unable to move. There had to be a logical explanation for these events. Yes, but what? Again, she felt Michael's presence. With her newly found faith in herself, she knew for whatever reason, he had come to her assistance again just when she needed him most. She was at peace.

Friday night was normally a lonely night. The kids were off on dates. Roy was at his regular poker game, and Maggie was alone on line with friends via the computer. Not this Friday night. She was determined she and Roy were going to celebrate. She could wear another new outfit, and know she was going to knock the world dead with her excitement. She had no idea of the disappointment and shock in store for her. Only her son, Brad, came home after school to change his clothes and inform her he was going on a very important date, which had been, as usual, a long time in the planning and he was unable to cancel. Nicole had left a note and called on the answering machine to say she was spending the night with Arlene, a close friend, to go to a rock concert and would be back Saturday or Sunday. A senior in high school, she thought she was grown and took liberties with authority like most people would change their minds about food in a cafeteria line. Maggie would deal with her later. Roy would be home soon, and she would set herself to pounce upon him.

Roy was almost like a comet in his predictability. He showed up at home right on time. Maggie was at the door in his face with her good news. "Roy, they offered me every-thing I wanted! Remember that I told you things were going to happen and now they have. I am going to Arkansas with a new position, new title, a raise, secretary and a new company car," she said as she danced around like a giddy teenager. "And WE are going out and celebrate. So, you can spend your winnings from previous poker games on me tonight."

Roy gave her a half smile, walked to the refrigerator for a beer, and said, "Maggie, we have to talk!"

"Sure I understand there will be many decisions that we will have to make. We can talk about them tomorrow. To-night I want to celebrate, dance and decide we are going to have a great life," she said as Brad gave her a kiss on the cheek as he passed her on his way out the door.

"No, Maggie, we really need to talk," Roy said, this time

with much more seriousness in his voice.

She could tell something was of deep concern to him and her mood quickly turned an about face.

"What's the problem Roy? I know that look when I see it. Aren't you happy for me? We are going to change, but the details can be worked out before I have to decide, and we can talk about it all weekend," she said as she came over to give him a hug, and he turned away.

"No, it's not as simple as that Maggie. There is never a convenient time or place to discuss this. Your life seems to be moving in a much more positive direction now, and I..., I want a divorce," Roy said.

The only sound that could be heard was from the clock in the hallway. The statement floored Maggie in her tracks. In almost a panic she thought he had found out about her affair with Michael. She simply asked, "Why?" and sat down in the nearest chair as her legs felt suddenly weak from shock.

"I can't say how, what, or exactly when it happened, but our love left sometime back. I needed attention and found it with someone else. I'm sorry it has to be this way. You haven't done anything wrong, and I'm feeling as guilty as the sin I am accusing myself of, and can't find a better time to bring this up than now. Your new promotion seems to be the best opportunity to sadden you with this news. I am truly sorry, " Roy said. It was obvious his soul was also heartbroken.

He sat down himself and waited for her response. For several moments, neither could, nor chose to, move or make an utterance. Disbelief had filled the room like smoke rising from the quenching of the ashes of their marriage. Hundreds of thoughts raced through each of their minds. Maggie debated whether or not to pour herself a drink, and her numbed body moved toward the bar hoping one might be of benefit. Roy watched in surprise as she poured a scotch on the rocks.

"When did you start drinking scotch? " he inquired.

"People change their tastes, once in a while, or is that something new to you? " she said and breathed out a long sigh.

It was obvious Roy had anguished over his decision, for the better part of the week or longer. Oddly enough, Maggie felt sorry for his awkwardness and the guilt she knew he must have been feeling. At the same time, she wondered if he had found out about Michael and was leaving because of her misguided mistake. For some strange reason, it was hard to be angry, but the hurt was there regardless. She saw a positive opportunity in the face of this sea of negativity.

"Shit, Roy," she said. "You know, if it hadn't been this, it would have been something else, I suppose. Our marriage has been in the can for years I guess. In as much as you sprung the news on me, I have the right to respond. Oh, please don't take this personally, Roy, but this opportunity comes around so seldom and I really want to take full advantage," Maggie said gaining composure and her thoughts as she walked to her usual chair. Just then it dawned on her, just because this appeared to be bad, she had wanted her marriage to improve, it didn't mean she might have to stay with the same man and she began to relax.

"Nope, not going to sit in it. Lately I'm thinking better on my feet." She whirled around and with all the sincerity of a mother said, " Listen Roy, if you think you have found a new love in your life there are a few things you should really know in order not to fuck this one up too. Let me do you both a favor. Now listen very carefully. "With one look in her eyes, it was obvious her mind was totally in gear.

"Don't stop doing the little things you are currently doing for her, but you stopped doing for me years ago. Women, and men too for that matter, fall in love as much with your actions as anything else. You were more, as I am sure you are now with her, considerate of my feelings in the beginning. Let me see, just to pinpoint for much more clarity, you used to tell me how pretty I was. More over, you went to the details of the matter, my eyes, hair, even the way I walked. Those things made me feel special Roy, as I am sure it now makes her feel special. You stopped to think of me in the middle of the day, when a phone call meant so much. Not only was it a very pleasant surprise, but an obvious sign of your love and concern, letting me know I was on your mind, and feeling myself as important, just because you cared. You see, Roy, caring is what it is all about, in one form or another. We lost the caring somehow along the way." A tear began to form in her eye, but she quickly wiped it off and continued.

"Roy, caring is shown in ways we never think of till it's gone. Time! You had the time, as I am sure you make the time with your new love, but as the years went by, time with me, the kids and the family, as a unit, just slipped away. If I could pin point one of the greatest indications of a failing relationship, it's the lack of time dedicated to it. Time to talk like we used to do for hours, about things which seemed important, yet just filled in as glue to keep us talking because we enjoyed each other so. Time to share ourselves, the little things that made us feel unique to each other. Yes, Roy, we made the time then, even though we were always busy. Busy with this or busy with that, but never too busy to recapture the best of times before. In so doing, or not doing as the case may be, we let our lives drift away."

"Yes, and as it started to drift, we suffered more of the problems the incorrect use of our time created. Indifference! We just didn't seem to care to pick things up, make the corrections, and try harder. All along we felt an emptiness inside which was simply missing each other, and never recognized it at all." Tears were now flowing from Maggie's eyes, down her cheeks, and she turned away. There was much more to be said. "Don't get me wrong, Roy, you are not totally to blame. I share the faults. Now I am entitled to my opinions as to how it affected me. I missed the hugs, not the sex, but the hugs you gave when you knew I had experienced a bad day. That's what I missed and knowing the love was there, and the emptiness I felt knowing it was leaving. Women, your new love, and me need the sensitivity it provides to give us emotional support. So much for emotions, let's address the mental attitudes," she said as the tears vanished.

"Did you ever once hear what you constantly told me to put me down...Why can't you see! You shouldn't think that away, it's stupid! That's your opinion, but it's wrong! Little remarks like that made me feel small and worthless, just because they came from you. CREDIT Roy; give your new love credit for her ability to think for herself. You might not have meant to rob me, but you did every time you put me down, belittled my ideas, and insinuated you had the only grand ideas on the planet and mine were insignificant. Believe me, IT HURT ROY. Do it to your new love and you will be looking again. I never needed you, or anyone, to dictate to me the way I should feel and think. Your comments made me feel small."

"Now, Roy, let's talk physical. The sex was fabulous and I knew it was the very best I had ever experienced. With you, it seemed like time stood still, and Roy it did. For some reason those cherished ideals and ideas of tenderness, gentleness, excitement, and romance seemed to be frozen in time somewhere. Oh, every once in a while after the first few years it returned on occasion, but not often enough. Now, don't get me wrong here, this is not totally your fault, we just quit trying, grew too familiar, and became comfortable. When was the last time you gave me a passionate kiss like you did years ago? I miss it! And, oh, when you felt a little horny, I never refused you. Yes, wham bam, thank you ma'am and fall asleep ten minutes later while ignoring the emotions you had just started in me. Yes, Roy I'm sure you are now enjoying a great sex life with HER, but for how long? I needed to be shown I was loved physically, more times than I was. When I wanted to cuddle, you were hot, cold, tired, not in the mood, whatever it took to get rid of me, and yes, Roy, in TIME it took its toll. Remember, much later in your relationship being touched the same way as when love was new, still counts and is very much appreciated by a woman, and not for just your satisfaction."

   As she spoke, Roy began to think back over the things of which he had just been accused. Had he forgotten the little things? Had he been so negligent of being himself, the person he once was? He wondered. To his conception, he had given all he thought he had to give. Was that not enough? Had he failed so badly? Did his efforts not count for anything? As she began to express her views, he was suddenly forced to acknowledge they had never really known each other. In his confession, he knew it was too late to even try. He knew in his reality how he had once loved her. It had been real to him. Her voice brought back a fonder memory, and at the same time, left him empty. Was it the years, or the boredom? He just didn't know. Being taken for granted was a two way street, he thought, but he was in no position to argue now.

"Well, as much of a shock as this is to me, I can't blame you alone, for I too have been guilty of letting time cause me to forget the moments when our love was new and exciting. We, both you and I, are guilty of letting it waste away without putting up much effort to try and keep it together. I truly hope you are not surprised. I am not offering you any resistance in the form of anger, rage, resentment, or malice. Starting over is not so bad of a thing if one can get over the first stages of fright. Now this is not to say you can waltz out of this relationship without paying the costs involved. I'm not talking about the emotional costs, God knows you will have to go through those with HER holding your hand. I'm talking real money costs. You will pay for the divorce, pay me for half the equity in this house and other assets we jointly own. Also, any other costs related to this request I am sure you feel would make you the happiest man in the world. I wish you luck. As for me, I would prefer to be alone now, you go on to the poker game, your girlfriends, or wherever you wish to go. Just go," Maggie said as she turned to pour herself another scotch.

Roy was speechless as he sat with his mouth open. Whatever he had assumed from the Maggie he once knew, was not coming out of the Maggie who was standing in front of him. "We will have to talk about what we are going to do about the kids," he said in disbelief and an effort to adjust to the new Maggie.

"Sure we will, Roy, we've got the entire weekend to adjust. Now, go on about your business, I've got some reading which needs to be done and plans to be made. Oh, Roy, you're going to be all right, Hon, believe me. Don't think of it as if you were losing a wife, you aren't, you're just gaining a much closer friend," she said as she walked out of the room.

Maggie changed clothes and once again retreated to the park with THE GIFT in hand. It would not be long until dark, and she wanted to read those wonderful words just once more. She, too, was still in shock at the ease in which she had dealt with Roy's news. A smile came to her face as she realized she had met the challenge with the five ingredients of acceptance, blessing, gratitude, joy, and love. Roy was still going to be loved for all the things he had meant to Maggie over the years, it was just the love they once shared was not enough to hold them together. It was not worth the staying together to waste one life, much less two.

The weekend passed with amazing simplicity, both Maggie and Roy were nicer and more courteous than they had been for years. The kids had taken the news much better than expected. They were not children any more, and maybe in their own way, saw the marriage had managed to survive like a ghost, just putting up a front from time to time. Both Bradley and Nicole were going to finish school; Nicole would be graduating in a few months and then off to college. Brad had only one more year and then God knows what he had planned for his future. At any rate, he was going to stay with Roy and Nicole would go with Maggie after her graduation. Roy decided to take out a loan to give Maggie her share of the equity in their home and much to each other's surprise there was harmony. They even managed to save attorney's fees from the usual fight that ensued. Maggie really wanted Roy to be happy, because she knew exactly what he was going through, as she had felt the same way for some time. And to think it all began with a visit to the grocery. Michael had become a very special person in her life, even after his death, and for some strange reason, she often felt his presence from time to time. THE GIFT was much more than what most people would think. To Maggie it was a chance to start again. This time she would be able to look both forward and backward in life. The mistakes, which she had found brought her the most grief, were now stepping stones to a much brighter existence. She may find another love, but for now she had another life waiting ahead of her. The first thing Monday morning she would prepare for brand new tomorrows.

Monday there was a meeting called in the Lounge around ten o'clock and there seemed to be an air of excitement. The partners were waiting what she had to say after discussing the matter with her family. They were off the hook if for any reason Maggie could not go to Arkansas. Oh, they would have to offer her another position, but not one of such importance and open to the total financial picture of the firm. The first thing Maggie said was she had discussed the matter with her family and unfortunately there would be a divorce. There was a strong rush of silence in the room and the anticipation could be cut with a knife it was so thick.

Then she floored them with, "But that's the breaks in the business world, huh fellas!" She turned to Carl Williams and said, " Oh, by the way Carl, I know you will be writing letters of introduction to the new account. In as much as this news may be disappointing, it does have its good points. Please change my name in all your correspondence to them and in the future, I am taking back my maiden name. My full name as well. Here after and forever more, please refer to me as Susan Bagwell, Maggie just seems a bit immature and out of character. Besides, she just doesn't exist anymore."

THE AWAKENING

The afternoon sunshine was glaring through the huge penthouse window behind her desk. The brightness of the light bothered her eyes as it bounced off the Woman of the Year award in her trophy case. She had intended to move the thing a hundred times. Every day about the same time, she took out a special key, unlocked the lower right hand desk drawer and would take out THE GIFT. It was now a dirty worn envelope containing a few tattered and fading pages. She had read it so many times over the last ten years that she knew it all by heart, and didn't have to read it to repeat the words. She had come such a long way from the simple Maggie, she once was. She now was the powerful corporate figure of Susan Bagwell. Leaning back in her custom made, executive chair, she closed her eyes to rest them from the light and began to think about all that had happened since she had received THE GIFT. It had all happened so quickly. A one day loving affair with a stranger had changed her life.

She was a different person then as Maggie. Maggie always wanted something more out of life but was just shy of achieving her expectations. She was almost ready to surrender to not having anything until that fateful day when she learned how to focus on achieving everything she needed. All she had to do was to go within her own desires and make a clear statement of what she wanted. It was simple, or was it?

Her husband Roy solved her situation with the marriage when he asked her for a divorce. She even surprised herself at the calm ease with which she handled the news. Poor Roy... she felt sorry for him and guilty of her affair, but, at any rate, it turned out the way she wanted. Roy had never married the bimbo he left her for, but did eventually get remarried. Perhaps he married again to keep him company or to have someone to take care of Brad. Brad chose to live with his father during his last year in high school. She did not blame Brad. After Brad graduated and left for college, she never had any more contact with Roy. Her move to Arkansas had been difficult on her relationship with Brad. She had missed him terribly and kept as close to him as possible living a long distance away. But they each had to make their decisions on their own. Her opportunity was in front of her to start anew, and Brad had wanted to stay with his father and graduate with all his friends. Their daughter Nicole chose to go with her. She was going off to college, and it really didn't make a hill of beans one way or the other. Nicole had always been a free spirit, and it was her choice to go with her mother. It all seemed as if it were only yesterday, she thought as a smile came on her face and she remembered those first days at the chicken plant.

The bed at the motel, where she was staying, felt so uncomfortable even a few good hours of sleep was regarded as better than average. Considering the location of the account, Susan was lucky there was even a large enough town nearby to have a motel. She had orchestrated her arrival with a new name, outfit, hairstyle and attitude. Upon checking into the motel, she had the name, and her positive attitude pushed to the limits. It was obvious the fashionable outfit and hairstyle were totally out of the question. She found herself in the middle of "Hooterville", in the southern part of Arkansas, with an eighteen- year- old daughter who practiced complaining like it was an art form. It was bad enough she was from the north. She could not understand half the things these people said. It seemed like she could see the grits flying out of their mouth with every word. She decided she would make the best of the situation, thinking it had to get better. This was Friday, her first day in her new town and by Monday morning she would be ready for whatever came her way. Nicole wanted to go shopping and out of pure boredom she was ready for the challenge of the day.

"Hooterville", as she referred to it, didn't have a mall as such, she soon found out. So, they followed the crowd to the main hub of uptown shopping mania, the local Big W discount store. Nicole could have screamed, but Susan was going to make the best of it. She decided that it was a good time to spend with Nicole and would pick up some of the basic things every woman would need moving to a new town. It could have been being in a new location, or the store not stocking her usual brands, or Nicole's complaining, but her mood left her and frustration was not long in completely captivating her entire being. Bad enough she was actually ready to go back to the motel. Her mind was on a million other things as she started her car and began to back out of the parking space. She knew she had failed to look to see if the way was clear when the car jolted to a dead stop with a quick crashing sound. She waited for the male driver to get out of his truck. She figured he would come over and start to belittle her for being a "woman driver", and so she waited. Nicole just gave her mother a REAL SMART, MOTHER look, but knew better than to say it out loud.

"What's the matter with that asshole? Why doesn't he get out of his truck and come over here?" her voice angry as she opened her door and started walking back to his truck. With the mood she was in at the moment, each step brought her disposition to pinpoint sharpness. She made the mistake of starting to speak before reaching the window.

"Say, are you blind? Didn't you see me pulling out of my parking space, and why didn't you get out and survey the damage with me? Are you crippled too?" flew out of her mouth before he could get his window rolled down completely.

Much to her surprise, he was the most ruggedly handsome man she had seen in the entire town. Her expression and demeanor changed rapidly.

"Well, I was waiting on you to get out of your car. You seemed in such a hell of a hurry before I just wanted to give you some coolin off time," he clearly stated, slowly removing his sunglasses. "Is it really that bad?"

Then he spoke to another man passing by, "Say Charlie, look back there at this fender bender and tell me if there is any damage to this lady's (his eyes rolled over and looked her up and down) car." He smiled at her and said to Charlie, never mind my truck, just look at the car." He said looking back at the man on his way to look at the possible damage.

"Nah, Joe, ain't no damage to either of ya. Bumpers hit just right," the man said waving his hand as he turned to go.

"Well, looks like there's no damage done and we're blocking this aisle for the other customers." He reached up and put his sunglasses back on.

"I'm going to let you go first, I really would prefer to have you in front of me so I can keep an eye on what you might do next if you don't mind," he said as he started pulling his truck back out of the way.

"Wait, I'm really sorry, I'm new in town and....."

"I know, " he said with a smile.

She stuck out her hand to the window and said, " I'm Maggie Hobbs... No, no, that's not my name, it's...." she started to continue when he interrupted.

"Look lady, you are not having a very good day. You just hit my truck and you can't remember your name. Maybe, you'd better go back home, take a nap and get some rest." W i t h that, she had had enough and stomped away back to her car. She could hear his chuckle as she was leaving. What could she expect next? "Hooterville" was so far from the palace she had pictured in her dreams. It seemed to be a nightmare she felt she was living moment by moment. Well, at least the guy in the truck was attractive. Definitely above average, judging by what she had seen just riding around town. She was not going to allow the bump at the Big W, or the rest of the disappointments, ruin her attitude for the opportunity she had waiting ahead of her.

The plant was about twenty miles away in the next town, if one could call it a town. On the way to the plant, on a practice run, she soon found the perfect spot to escape the pressures and read THE GIFT. There was a feeder pond down a dirt road off the highway with a gigantic shade tree beside it. Just the place she could use to calmly read and lose herself from the pressures of the day. It was late Sunday afternoon and Nicole wanted to stay back at the motel and watch a movie, so Susan decided to venture under the tree alone after she found the plant.

A building the size of a poultry plant should be not hard to find. She knew it was on the road she was on, just not how far out. It was not long until she saw buildings that were most likely the one she wanted to find. She pulled her car into the main entrance and stopped the car, placing it in park while she gathered her thoughts. PINETREE POULTRY PROCESSING PLANT, were not the words that shocked her, it was the next line, Division of Damien Developments, that caused her heart to skip a beat, Michael's memory was alive again. She slowly turned around and drove back to the pond she had admired.

When she found it again, there was just enough room on the side of the road to park her car. The fence gate was fastened with heavy duty wire, which gave her a bit of a problem at first. All she could think of was the coolness and serenity she hoped to find resting beneath the tree's huge long branches. Those thoughts were more than obvious, for while she was walking in the tall fescue grass she failed to notice the enormous piles the cows had left behind. Before she knew it, she was ankle deep in manure. It was as awful smelling as she thought, but she found it was much more slippery than she could have imagined. Between the position she had gotten herself into and the wetness of the grass, she twisted one time too quickly and found herself crashing to her butt. Now, she not only had her shoe covered with what a cow discarded, but her hands and clothes were equally proportioned. As if that was not enough, the chiggers and mosquitoes were delightfully chewing away at her lily white skin. It was not something she was the least bit knowledgeable about.

"Damn to hell! " she said in total frustration, when about that same time there came the sound of uncontrollable laughter.

"You look like you're in a hell of a spot Missy," a voice called. She looked around and right there next to the tree stood a farmer. She could only assume he was a farmer by his attire. His laughter continued until she was once again on her feet.

"That's not very polite," she snapped, "Do you always laugh at women who fall down on your property? Why you are lucky you've not been sued."

"I don't worry too much about it Missy. You must have missed the NO TRESPASSING SIGNS, and I learned after moving here about painting the top of the fence post a God awful purple color to warn away those who can't read. It's a native custom 'round these parts. I take it you ain't from around here either. Besides, if you'd have come up and asked, I'd warned you about the dangers involved around my pond." he calmly stated.

She began to see the humor of her position and smiled. "Dangers? There are more than fallen in 'this stuff'?"

"Sure are ma'am. You could have stumbled on Ole Slick, a som bitch of a copperhead, that's a snake if you didn't know. Or, ya might be allergic to that broad leave patch of poison oak you just fell into."

Susan's eyes got as big as coffee cups and before she could catch herself in desperation, out of her mouth came the most moanfull "Oh Shit!" the saddest of souls could utter.

Again, the farmer saw it so funny he found himself unable to control his laughter, although he knew the seriousness of her situation.

"Look Missy, before you wind up in some really serious trouble, come on down behind the dam here and ride with me on the tractor to the house. My wife can lend you a hand with those clothes and get rid of the poison oak oil, that is, if you don't mind. But you'll wish ya had of tomorrow if ya don't," the farmer said with a grin.

"I'll accept your kindness, but won't your wife have a different opinion about you bringing home a strange woman in the late afternoon," she shouted as she followed him down the incline of the dam.

"Obviously, you haven't met and don't know my Katron. She welcomes everyone and she is said to have the ability to look at a person and see clear to his or her soul. If she don't like ya, there ain't much hope for ya," he said climbing into the cab of an old tractor. "Oh, by the way, my name is Charlie, Missy. You got another name you'd rather be called?"

"Missy is just fine Charlie. My name was Maggie but I changed it to Susan during my divorce, but to be honest it hasn't been long and I'm not used to being called Susan just yet." she said from the back of the tractor as she grabbed for his shoulders as it started chugging toward the farm house.

Charlie was tall and, other than the few words he said between his laughter back at the pond, he never said another thing as they made their way to the house. Susan felt embarrassed to even see another person, much less a stranger, but Charlie's words about the poison oak and the blackish green slim all over her person seemed to persuade her to give in and swallow her pride. There was also something else about him that she intuitively liked, despite his laughter at her, and she could also not afford to go to the plant in the morning all itching and red from poison oak. What kind of first impression would she make? She could just imagine, too, the smell this stuff would leave in her new company car. Charlie tried to make her go inside, but she was steadfast not to just simply barge into another woman's house without first being invited. Charlie, being a man, would not know of such unspoken consent between women. Try as he would, she held her ground and soon, there in the threshold, suddenly stood a tall slender woman who's understanding smile welcomed Susan into her home. There seemed to be something special in the warmth of her eyes and the curve of her smile.

"Ma, Missy here met up with a bit of a problem down at the pond and I told her you'd come to her rescue." Charlie said turning to Susan. "Now, you been introduced. If ya wanna stay out here all day, it's OK by me. I'm fixin to go to the barn," he turned and started walking away.

Katron moved toward Susan and extended her hand, then saw, and got a whiff, of what had happened.

"My my Maggie, you are a sight. Let's get those clothes off of ya and into the washer. I think I surely have something you can wear," Katron said as she motioned toward the porch door.

"It's a good thing you happened to come up to Charlie's pond. People round here don't cotton to strangers, especially Yankee ones. We've lived her for ten years or so, I reckon, and they still just tolerate us. Don't guess we will really fit in as real locals. People from this area think one way; a person is either one of them, or a Damn Yankee. It really don't make much difference where you come from in reality."

There just happened to be a wash room just off the porch, perhaps to allow Charlie to get the same stuff off him before he entered the house. Katron pointed to it and said, "Now you go in there, take off all your clothes Maggie, and I'll bring you a thick robe to wear. You take a shower and I'll put those clothes in to wash. Don't worry, we have two water heaters so it won't scald you while the washer is using hot water."

She did as she was told, and it felt good being taken care of again. As she was changing, she realized Katron had called her Maggie and she had not been told her name. She had never been so glad to be close to soap and a hot shower in her life. Katron had placed the robe and a new towel on the sink in the small room and was inside the kitchen when Susan emerged from the bathroom.

"I'm in here, Maggie, making some iced tea. Won't you please come join me?" she shouted. As Susan entered the home for the first time she felt a friendly comfort engulf her.

"Katron, this is extremely hospitable of you and I want you to know I am forever in your debt." As Katron motioned her to sit at the table, Susan said, "I don't mean to sound rude, but you called me Maggie and Charlie didn't introduce me. How did you know my name? " Susan asked.

"Isn't it Maggie? You kinda put out a feeling that was your name," Katron said smiling, never stopping from her work at the stove.

"Yes, it was, until recently after my divorce. Now, I'm using my middle name Susan, I just thought it was strange that you would call me Maggie with such ease."

"Oh, you can't see it, I forgot!" Katron said as she turned from the stove and looked at Susan. "Or maybe it is just so new to you it is not being felt easily, " she turned back and continued with the tea.

"Felt WHAT?" Susan said.

"Why, the GIFT you got! You're special honey. I could feel it before you came in from the field with Charlie," she said bringing in the tea and setting it down on the kitchen table. "And don't let Charlie scare ya or make ya feel uneasy. When we first moved down here he was put down so many times, and had to make adjustments, sometimes I think he's becoming one of the old farts himself," she grinned.

"Oh, forgive me too, some people around here think I'm a might touched, but truth is I got a special gift myself, got it from my grandmother. I can kinda feel things, and you honey gotta a gift of some kind," she said, so matter-of-factly.

Susan just sat there for a moment, trying to take all this in and absorb what Katron was saying. "Well, that's nice, mind telling me just what kind of gift I got?" she asked.

"Don't really know, Hon," Katron started. "Ya see, some folks are born with a gift and some kinda have to wait till they are ready to handle it. You musta had to wait, cause I can tell it's just birthin out of you. So, how did ya come to be down here?" she asked, as if her statement was just about the weather, as she poured the tea.

Susan almost had an intuitive nature about Katron. Somehow, as she remembered both the strangers, Joseph and Father Shawn, who had helped, she felt their meeting was not by mere happenstance. "It's a strange situation. I met someone who gave me something he had for many years. He called it a gift too," Susan said slowly.

"Was it in writing?" Katron asked, " Never known it to be in writing. Most times you just get it and somebody has to explain it to ya."

"Well, you've totally taken me off guard, Katron. I'm not from a place where such things are explained. Perhaps you can lend me a bit of your knowledge of such mysteries?" Susan inquired slowly.

"Can't Maggie, I don't know what it is ya got, only know ya got something. Now, you will be findin out more and more as time takes ya where you are supposed to be, and I'll be here to help if I can," she noted while getting up to check on the washing machine. They would soon become the best of friends. Susan would soon learn the ins and outs of Arkansas country living from Katron. She was a big help too. She nagged Charlie until he got the pond grass, mostly weeds, mowed so the snakes could at least be seen. She even made him fix a place for Susan to visit under the tree and read. She knew it was the surest way to get her to come back to visit. And Susan did go to the pond on a regular basis, to read and re-read THE GIFT and to learn from Katron.

Susan felt herself drifting off to sleep as she relived those first days on her own with the new job there in "Hooterville". A smile came to her face when she recalled the first visit to the chicken processing plant. She had gotten up the next morning, put on the new outfit and dressed to the nines. The facility was actually much better than she had expected. The building was about three stories. It had a stained glass front with concrete columns supporting a huge entranceway. But to her, it was in Arkansas, the country, and away from her idea of civilization. She was early as she recalled, and knew they should be expecting her. After all, her firm had handled their advertising business for years. Not only was it worth millions, they were like one of the family. Soon she learned it was only because of a certain stockholder, and his wealth, Susan had this opportunity. All of course would change with Michael's passing. She realized she was on her own and that would soon present itself.

She walked up to the receptionist desk and announced, "I'm Susan Bagwell, and I am here to see Mr. Joseph Butler, I have an appointment at nine and I'm early, " she said almost boastfully.

"Then you'll have to wait till it's your turn, I guess. He's having coffee with the skipper of the safety crew. Won't be long. They been going at it about an hour," the secretary replied turning. " Oh, you can go down to the cafeteria and get you a cup of coffee, if ya like. Need any change?" she said, as she went about her business.

"No thank you, I'll just have a seat here and wait," Susan said sitting down on a long waiting room sofa.

"Suit yourself," she said and she was back at work. Susan was expecting a warmer reception, but did not let it dull her confidence. About thirty minutes later the phone rang, and the secretary told Mr. Butler about Susan being in the lobby waiting.

"Ms. Bagwell, Mr. Butler totally forgot about your morning appointment, and will see you right away. Go all the way down this hall. His office is the last door on your right. He is expecting you now," she said with a hand motion and was back at work.

She walked down to the open door. She found another secretary in a smaller office, who greeted her much more warmly than had the first. She motioned her to go on inside the door to his office. When she walked in, there was a familiarity with Mr. Butler's office. Something special was there, but she could not put her finger on it. Mr. Butler was on the phone, with his back to her, and surprisingly he was in a wheel chair. He ended the conversation, and began to speak as he turned. Their expressions could never have been more alike, for they had just met a few days before in the Big W parking lot.

"Well, it's you! I am crippled you see. That's why I didn't get out of the truck," he said smiling and extending his hand out to greet her. " I trust you took my advice, got some rest and can now remember your name," he said, as his smile got broader. She was totally taken back by her action at their first meeting and he could tell. " You see, in a small town, you never know just who you will 'run-in-to'. Just consider it your first lesson of Arkansas living."

Susan's day was shot. How was she going to live it down, with what she had done at the Big W store? She found honesty to be the best policy.

"Well, hell, next time tell somebody so they don't make a complete ass out of themselves," she said as her hand went out to meet his.

There was a comforting warmth in his grip, a welcoming which was not one of a normal nature, and she was at peace and knew she was forgiven. It was not the first time she had made such a mistake; however, this time there was a great deal more remorse for her actions, and a lot more at stake. As it turned out, things could not have worked out any better because of the conditions Susan would be under. Although she was in charge of the account, the owners of the poultry company hardly accepted her. They were from the South and a Yankee woman in charge of their advertising was not at all satisfactory. Joe was the liaison between the company and Susan. Her willingness to work hard was no trade off in their opinion for her radical ideas for the company. As soon as Michael Damien's estate was settled, there were going to be changes in the public relations account personnel, or it was their general outlook. Then there was THAT secretary, or assistant, Susan had hired. It was one thing to send a woman down to handle the account, but to have her hire THAT girl, THAT disrespectful, smart ass Yankee.

Susan had done her homework with what she thought she would need to counter some of the unforeseen problems in this mans' world. She had gone to employment agencies, newspaper ads, and even the personnel office of the company to find just the right person to work with her. The results were less than pitiful. Then one day while Susan was near the reception desk, Nancy walked in, lost and asking for directions. She was tall and slender. Her green eyes and auburn hair caused heads to turn, from the lawn maintenance crew to the copy room girls. There was also something in her walk which created a respect for her long before she got to her destination. Her manner was pure "Yankee" and set a bad taste in the mouths of the plant officials, which would not leave till she did. After efforts failed to get directions, she must have seen something she liked enough to want to stay.

"Excuse me!" were the next words out of Nancy's mouth. "Please direct me to your personnel department, or do you call it resource management?" she said with a half sarcastic grin.

"I'm sorry, we are not hiring at the moment," the receptionist answered back.

"How would you know, Toots, I ain't talking about pluck'en no chickens, babe. I'm in executive management," she said with a bit more impatience this time.

To which the secretary came back, " I told you, we are not hiring at this time, and I am going to call security," the girl said with a quiver in her voice.

"I don't need a job with them, but if they got an ounce of brains more than you, bring 'em on." Just then the receptionist picked up the phone and dialed the security command. Susan interrupted quickly.

"That's all right, I'll handle this matter, I'm Susan Bagwell," she said extending her hand, "And what part of New York are you from Ms.?"

"Queens, Ms. Bagwell, and I'm Nancy Pharr. They got more here like you, this place just might survive!" and they began to walk back to Susan's office.

Nancy was not only extremely attractive; she was equally intelligent in organizing and implementation. Her rough exterior manners, not to mention her orientation as a Yankee, had set a few strikes against her. Susan was impressed with her ability to communicate with the greatest of ease, but it was no wonder. Her references were impeccable and she would have been at her last position if she had not had one too many drinks and married a good looking Marine officer one night. She thought this was her dream lover till she got to the base he was transferred to in Arkansas. Once here, she found she had just had one too many of one or both of them. She was not meant to be a Marine's wife, living in a base home in the middle of nowhere. So, she left Lt. Sexy and was simply headed anywhere he wasn't. Susan was comfortable with the relationship with Joe Butler, but needed someone on her side all the time, all the way. Nancy was going to turn out to be one of a very select group of her friends who would play a significant part in what THE GIFT had in store for Susan.

Returning to the present.... The sun had now changed its position and was no longer bouncing off the Woman of the Year award as it caught Susan's eye. She had seldom taken the liberty of day dreaming over the last ten years. She used her day dreaming time while in meditation with THE GIFT. It was never wasted time. She thought about how she had, or thought she had, set out her goals, never knowing the time it took to achieve them also served her a very valuable lesson. The very first few weeks at the plant were difficult, to say the least, and eased up some when Nicole finally started college. The long days of summer's end had given her ample time to spend at the pond reflecting on who she was and who she wanted to become. Katron had ridden Charlie's back till he had not only cleared a comfortable space, but also had gone so far as to build a table and chairs. Not only had Charlie cut the grass around the pond, almost to the dirt, he had set out insect traps and pesticides. Katron was well aware that the mosquitoes, chiggers, and ticks would soon change Susan's mind about coming back if she had to continually slap the bugs off. Susan never knew for sure whether it was Katron's prodding or Charlie's kindness, but there was always a pitcher of iced tea and several glasses in an ice chest sitting beside the table. Charlie would never have admitted to making it on his own, he was just that kind of man. It was just after Nicole had left that a very special thing happened to Susan as Katron and she sat in the cool shade of the huge tree by the pond. It was one day when Katron became more than a friend; she became a mentor.

"I had a long dream about you last night, Susan," Katron said looking to the western sunset.

"Oh, not a nightmare I trust," Susan joked.

"No, it was more like a vision than a dream. You were

walking, or being lead by a tall man, gray hair and the deepest blue eyes I've ever seen. You seemed to care for him, or were very secure in his leading, as you never questioned his guidance. It started with such bliss, I myself felt an immense amount of pleasure, and then it ended quickly. He was gone, but before he left he turned and faced me and said to assure you THE GIFT was there to give you everything that you truly desired. That you were not to be concerned about where it would take you or who was to be the next recipient, for it was ordained before it was given to you," and she turned and looked at Susan.

She knew that Susan knew exactly what the dream meant by the look on her face.

"I have learned over the years not to pry or question things which just come to me, it never did a bit of good, or bad for that matter, just to take things as they came, but I can tell you, there was a feeling of destiny in that vision, and I got the feeling this would not be the last one," Susan took Katron's hand and said, "Funny you should tell me now, for there has been a great weight on me as to what I was to do. I can't disclose all the details, but without knowing what it is, I know what you are saying is true, and I also know meeting you, and Charlie of course, was no mistake. I too know you are part of this destiny for some reason."

As she took her time on the ride home, Susan knew whatever might come her way; there would always be a Katron to be there for her. She just didn't know that there were always several out there waiting to help her make sure that her destiny was fulfilled. She would need all the help she could muster, for the hardest road of her life to that point, lay just ahead. The opportunity was lain at her feet to become everything she wanted to be. Now was the time she would need to prove herself to others who would present barriers on her journey. Little did she know that the new found friends in Arkansas were to become the tools she had to have to reach her goals. That each one had been sent to provide those areas where she was lacking. With only those few, she was set to build the dreams and, in a matter of time, she would come to realize. Early one morning the bombshell would be dropped, and it was up to her to prevent it from hitting its target.

Susan had only been at the plant for a few months. Just enough time to orient herself to the officers in charge and the operation of the business. She had been given a small office and she had never really felt extremely comfortable in, not only with the location, but the lack of privacy. Joe Butler was a company man down to the last detail, or appeared to be. He had opened up to her, and through his guidance, had helped her avoid several pitfalls management had provided. She was called to his office and this time his hands were being tied. It was Susan alone who would have to stand now on her own.

"Susan, the company has given you ninety days to make substantial increases in the results of the company's marketing plans," he said with a look of helplessness. "This is a 'good ole boy' organization and the time for female leadership just has not arrived. To be blunt, they want you to fall on your ass, and if a word of this ever got out I even hinted to you about their wishes, my ass would be there to serve as a cushion for you to land on."

Susan just smiled. " I knew this would ultimately happen, and it really is very lonely at the top. I think my own company wanted to see the same thing. I can turn it around, but I can't do it alone. Nancy is tops at organization, I know what I have to do, but there is one person mandatory to have on my side if I am to pull this off in ninety days... YOU! " and she sat down.

"ME....? Wait a minute, I was only giving you a warning what was down the road, not a plea for enlistment in your force. And besides, teaming up with you could mean a quick end to my career here, win or lose," Joe said fumbling around with papers on his desk so his eyes wouldn't meet Susan's.

She recalled everything she knew about him, both from his story and what she had heard in the plant. Joe had been on two tours of duty in Vietnam. He was a hero the first time and came back with several metals and stars on his chest. The problem was at the time, he did not have a lick of brains in his head. His old girlfriend was pushing to get married and he had seen the true light of what might happen if he was not so lucky to come back in one piece so he jumped at the offer. He was right about the not coming back. He stepped on a land mine and lost both his legs over there, just below the knees, while over here he was losing his wife. She also didn't have a brain and only saw a hero, never the reality of what war could do to a man. The mental effects didn't help to lessen the tension between them, and six months after being home, she was divorced and on her way to a much more exciting life, or so she thought. This experience, and the fact he was crippled, left Joe with a bitter taste for women. Then Susan came, but it was another part of Susan. It was Maggie he saw, never the hard driving Susan, until now.

Susan sat back, crossed her legs, looked at Joe, and deciding to play her trump card said, "Joe are you happy? I mean truly happy."

And with this Joe just gave her a perplexing look and quickly answered with a question,

"Who the hell is?"

Susan knew to what limits she could go, and she was not totally sure if it was meant for him to be the one. For some reason, she knew she had to speak frankly and truthfully to motivate him. She needed him on her side. After all, if he was against her, it would be a losing proposition all the way.

"Glad you asked, I am. Oh, not because of the circumstances or conditions around me, not because I am so damned lucky, and certainly not because I deserve it, but because I will it to be so." She got up and paced around the room.

"There was a time when all I could recognize was I WAS NOT happy. And I WAS NOT willing to do anything about it. Then, because of a strange twist of fate, I realized I was EXACTLY what I wanted to be. I had to accept it because I was the one who created the condition to begin with and was too lazy to take the time to make the necessary moves to change things to my advantage. You, Joe, may be in the same fix. I have only one way to look at things now. I have come a long way from where I was and I have just started my journey. I AM going to make my goals come true and have a much longer way to go, but I know I AM going to succeed in my quest. It's that simple. I will not give up after starting what I know I can achieve. You, on the other hand, are at the crossroads. With what you just told me, YOU put your career on the line, for mine. Now, the decision is up to you to be what you want, for good or bad. You alone have the power to make things in your life change. I want you to know it is clearly your choice, to support me. I will share with you the bounty of the rewards and believe me, rewards there will be and in amounts beyond your conception. It's up to you and a decision is not needed now, but within the next few days," and she turned and walked out the door hoping she had done the right thing.

Susan knew in order to make things come out far beyond her advantage she would have to go within deeper than she had before. She was off to the pond with THE GIFT in hand. It was an unusually warm day, one of those beautiful autumn days when you would enjoy doing anything else but what you had to do. She read and read again, but her concentration was not there, I AM going to do the best job this company has ever seen. I AM going to increase advertising results beyond what they have ever been. I AM able to accomplish this goal with ease. I AM going to figure out how to do this by morning, she thought to herself and then said it out loud. With the ending of those words, a calm had overtaken her. She closed her eyes and began to seek the inner most parts of her soul. Unlike any time before, she was now transported to another realm in her existence. Such peace was felt for a moment and she stopped to bask in the overall joy. Then a voice spoke, "Your desires are fulfilled!"

She was so startled and, in an instant she was back in reality at the pond. Such a positive attitude filled her she couldn't help but shout. Little did she know Katron had seen her and was nearly there to meet her.

"Heavenly day's child! Did you see Old Slick or something?" Katron said with a bit of shock.

"No Katron, I'm extremely happy, I just went deeper inside myself than I have ever gone and it felt so wonderful." Susan said getting out of the chair to embrace Katron. "I have a major problem and I have just been assured the answer is already here, but I'm not sure what it is just yet."

"Wish I could help," Katron said, "I only know I can only

try the things that I hadn't tried before to get things to work for me."

"That's it, Katron! That's it! Whatever worked before, might not have gotten the results. Those results may just come from the ones they omitted in the campaigns before." Susan said walking around in the deepest of thoughts. "Why didn't I recognize it? Why didn't I just come to you in the first place? Well, I've got to run. You just gave me the answer and you never even knew it," and Susan was off back to the office.

The next morning Joe wheeled into the office and told Susan he had given much thought to her comments. He was not sure why he came to the decision to go with her, but that even though it might mean his job, he was ready to go for it with everything he had. The truth was he had not been satisfied with his job at the plant for years and he saw his opportunity to venture into something much more exciting. He did find Susan much more exciting but somehow never found the right words, place or time to tell her. It was too late now; Susan smiled, hugged him and called Nancy into the office.

"We have only got ninety days to come up with a campaign to break all previous sales records. Joe, I want you to help Nancy get every file of all advertising this place has done for the last five, no ten years, and I mean everything, newspapers, radio, T V, direct mail, coupons, point of sale. I don't care what it is; I want it all and need it in ratio of sales to spots run in thirty-day results. We are going to stick our necks out. My agency had this account on a special basis. I can't expect any help from them. They want to see me gone and so do these plant assholes. We are on our own. This time we are going to do the things they didn't do. Most of the partners in the firm handled this account and have forgotten what's it like to have to hustle. WE have not forgotten, and by damn, we are going to make it work. If we do, others will be beating down our door and that door will have a new name on the shingle. Now, get our butts in gear and let's get it done. I've got to get in touch with some national contacts and make sure the space and placement is available."

Nancy and Joe worked well together. It took some hard looking but every ad campaign and the thirty-day sales results were compiled in less than five days. It looked as if coupons and TV back up produced the greatest amount of sales by far. It should, it cost the greatest amount of money, so the net figures were not that great on the bottom line. But they now had a figure to shoot for as their goal.

Most all the areas had been tried, point of sale and radio had not. For some reason the partners at the firm enjoyed the big splash and hoopla to impress the clients, after all it was their money. Point of sale promos and radio were the old way of doing the business and strictly for the new kids on the block. Susan knew in reality, they were now the new kids and this time, playing for all the marbles. It had only been a few days since all the material had been gathered. Before them were all the records of every ad campaign that had ever been done. There it was, right in front of their eyes, the answer. The point of sale coupons and radio was going to be the way. Now, all they needed was to come up with an exceptionally unique way to show off their combined talents.

The last two nights at Nancy's apartment hadn't given them the edge they were looking for. They seemed to be moving against a brick wall. The next day Nancy had to leave town and Joe was coming over to Susan's to work. She had to move fast, Nicole was at college and the place was a mess. She worked physically hard for the two hours prior to his coming over and swore she did not know why. Joe hadn't given her any reason to have any romantic thoughts toward him, but the idea of him coming over made things different somehow. Even the thought of what she was going to wear was back. Seemed like such a long time since she had dressed for a man, but it felt good. But Joe? No Way, she thought. She was not nearly ready for any more complications in her life. Besides, the fight of the century was about to take place and they would be concentrating. It was going to be strictly business, she thought.

Joe arrived at five and they went right to work, but neither of them had anything to offer, the wall was still there, so they just began to visit. She knew Joe was a beer drinker, so she had provided an ample supply of his favorite, Keystone Light. She gave the beer a try and, to her surprise enjoyed the taste, something she had never enjoyed before. As it was, the most natural reaction to beer eventually came about and she excused herself and went to the bathroom. It was the second time she had to excuse herself when she wondered how he was able to avoid the bathroom.

"How is it I'm only a middleman, or person, and you don't have to get rid of yours?" she asked half way smiling and feeling the effects about that time.

"Well, I'm glad you asked. The fact is I do, but don't know if your bathroom door is wide enough for my chair," he responded. She was in shock. She never considered what complications it might bring.

"Well, hell, let's just see!" she responded and they were off down the hall. Sure enough, the door was too small.

"Well, hell! I'm going to need your help. You chicken to help me inside?" was his reply.

Her bathroom was not equipped in anyway to accommodate the handicapped, but her last remark had fallen on her like cold honey and she now knew it was do it or else. "Sure Sport, I ain't chicken if you ain't," and she positioned herself to help him from the chair. Something had just happened that each of them instantaneously became aware of. The brick wall had just been torn down. Joe was tall and slender and knew just how to position himself to distribute his weight. She enjoyed the touch of his arms around her shoulders and his cologne caught her attention. The distance to the toilet was not that far, but it seemed each one of them wanted to make the trip longer than was required. Then they were there.

"I draw the line at bedpans and zippers. The rest, you are on your own," she said turning to leave, "I'll be right outside," and the door was closed.

As much as he wanted to relieve himself, Joe was thinking about the last few minutes. That pleasure had been long overdue. When he was done he shouted a quick "Okay," and the door quickly swung open. Each started to speak at the same time, the same words,

"Hey, I've got an idea..." and the laughter began. Each had seen the same thought at the moment.

"Go ahead!" she said laughing.

"We're chicken, but you're not", he said and she smiled. "My thoughts exactly, and now we have our radio spots." This time it took a bit longer to help Joe back to his chair. As Susan helped him in the chair, because of the small room, their faces met. For only a matter of time there was a question of what was to come next. Their lips slowly found the other's. Once again there was another memory. Once again there was the return of lost feelings. Soon it ended.

"I'm sorry," Joe said. "The moment of joy just overcame me, but it was something I have not experienced in years, and I am not one to pass up opportunity. Besides I gambled on you to begin with." This set her back, for she too had very much enjoyed the moment. What was the next step? She wondered. Before them was the turning point of a career, and also in front of her was something she too did not want to discard.

"It was indeed, very enjoyable for me too, but like they say 'When you're hot you're hot'. Let's concentrate on what's here for now," and she started to the living room.

As they got back to work, ideas seem to flow a dime a dozen, first one then another. The fire was there in more ways than one. This time the mark was going to be made forever. Joe suggested it should be on areas the company had never considered. There was a portion pack that was sold for less money because it was made up of miss cut pieces from the filet packs that were sold at premium prices. "What if we started a new production line, exclusively for the processing of the best parts of those mistakes and called them 'Deluxe Cuts'? They could be used for salads, soups, whatever." The lights began to come on and within just minutes the dare was made. "The customers would be 'chicken' if they did not try 'our chicken'." Then the light was out on their idea frenzy, and it was time for Joe to leave.

"Well, it's a done deal, and you can stick a fork in me, cause I'm done too. Time to head home," he said moving his chair away and toward the door. Joe wanted to stay longer. He just did not have the thoughts to make an excuse, or if he did, the words would not come out the way he wanted them.

He had more than simply enjoyed her company. It was more than business, yet he saw himself not enough for Susan. He just cussed to himself and figured leaving was best at the time.

"I'll walk you to the truck. I never thought it would have come by way of a bathroom," Susan said following behind him. Both of them wanted to avoid the leaving. Each had experienced excitement they never had counted on, with the project and with each other. Joe backed out of his space, turned and gave a smiling wave, and started home. Susan walked back to her apartment thinking a thousand thoughts. The kiss from Joe drifted through her mind and she smiled. It had been the first kiss in months and it felt warm, sincere and was overdue. That night she went to bed exceptionally early. The sun had not gone completely down, but the load of the last few days had tired her. A hundred thoughts crowded her mind as she began to feel herself fading off to sleep. For some reason she had closed the door to her bedroom, and noticed a break in the light of the setting sun from the front window. Someone was there in her apartment, standing in her bedroom doorway. Her heart began to beat and fear quickly captured her with cold emotion.

"Who's there? I have a gun," she said in a monotone voice hoping not to appear frightened.

"It's okay Maggie," came back from the other side of the door. The movement of the door began to create the usual hum of the twisting hinges. The light from the sun was just enough to darken his face, but the voice was familiar. For some reason her tenseness seemed to lessen, but the fear was still there. "Don't be afraid, you have nothing to fear," the voice called out. "You called to me and I'm here to answer, I told you I would always be here." She recognized the voice and her heart jumped. She knew it was Michael, but how? He moved a few feet closer to the edge of the bed post. In an admiring way, she thought she heard him release a long breath, perhaps with a tone of a friend long missed.

"But how...you are...you can't be...." she started to speak and he interrupted her quickly.

"That's really not important now is it Maggie? I've not very long and I want to assure you of something very important."

She sat up in the bed and patted the mattress next to her as if to motion for him to come there. By now her heart had not changed its beats but the rhythms were altogether different. He moved forward and sat down beside her. The light from the window over her bed allowed just enough illumination to see the sparkle in his eyes and the smile on his face.

"Oh, Michael, hold me," she said, as she reached for him. There was no time for thinking, he was there and that was all there was to her. His arms soon found their way around her tiny frame and she began to relax instantly. She started to cry. She was Maggie again and more than welcomed the memory of his touch and tenderness. He began to speak in the voice, low and calming.

"I know what these past months have been for you. Your heart has held an empty spot you long to fill. There is someone that also longs to be there. Someone that is just what you have created in your secret thoughts, though you know it not. Again, I remind you, time can't be rushed and again you must test your patience with waiting. Have you not seen the many things it has brought you so far? Has not your faith in yourself been enhanced enough to know whatever you need will be but a relatively short time in coming? I am sure you were selected to receive THE GIFT for that very purpose. You are now, as well as always, loved."

Maggie began to lean back against her pillows as she brought Michael down with her arms. As he slowly began to move his lips closer to hers, the alarm began to sound music. Her arms were empty. She was only dreaming. The radio was quickly shut off and she tried in vain to drift off to sleep, to recapture the dream, and the wonderful feeling it brought.

Slightly overcome by the experience of her dream, Susan bounded off to work early. She was excited at the possibilities she and Joe had conceived the previous night. It was going to take every bit of imagination that she, Joe and Nancy could muster to put this new ad campaign together. To be sure, she knew it would outdo profits than from any previous attempt.

"Okay, coffee is made, donuts are fresh and there aren't any excuses why we can't come up with a winning idea," she said. They had gone over the 'chicken' idea with Nancy. Nancy felt it was the way to go, basically because her mind had gone blank long ago. She was an implementor and organizer and whatever they gave her she knew she could make work, regardless. Susan knew the creativity would have to come from her. Joe would make sure the production and processing would be ready to meet the demand. It was comforting to know all she had to do was to get the final drafts. It was in just a few minutes the words began to flow.

"We know we're chicken. We think you might not be! We double dog dare you to try our new Deluxe Cuts Pieces for soups, salads, or your own creation for the very best you have to offer, from the very best we have to offer. Take the coupon at the market and if you don't like it, we'll buy it back. We are so confident you will, we ask you to send in how you used it, and you could win a thousand Cluck Bucks to purchase any of our products."

It was perfect and just corny enough to work. Throw out the challenge with a no-risk guarantee, then come up with a funny sounding reward. Percentages forecast many will buy and never even take the coupon. A smaller percentage will save the "original" receipt and bother to go through the trouble of mailing it in, and moreover, a high percentage will send in recipes for the $1,000 prize. It was nothing like the partners in the firm had ever done.

The next few weeks were extremely hectic for the three-some. Deadlines for radio productions had to be pushed to the limit. Susan had learned how to get around most any problem with a few gifts in the right places. Nancy was a whiz at the staggering of cross-country stations and getting the coupons prepared for distribution. The design department was told to put everything else on hold, with a bit of pressure, and produced the point of sale displays in record time. One day it seemed each one of the trio had a major problem which seemed impossible to correct and discouragement was obviously hidden behind their eyes. The problems were those that only each one could solve and this time there was no help from the others. Susan called Joe and Nancy into her office at the end of the day, recognizing something had to be done to quell this obstacle each was facing at a time when it would be most detrimental.

"I want us to look," she said, waiting for their replies. Joe and Nancy looked at each other in puzzlement and almost in harmony said, "Look at what?"

Susan began to speak in the tone of a mother guiding her

children to find the answers to their problems themselves,
"Look at what we have done so far. Look at the problems and
the situations we have overcome. Look at the way we have
pulled this thing together in a short period of time. We don't
have to think we can do it, simply because we know we've
already done it. Our faith in each other and the idea is enough.
Now, I see us succeeding in a magnificent way. The numbers
are coming in just as high as we knew they would be. But in
order for this to happen, we must all see them. I mean see
them clearly, distinctively, and not as if it were to come, but
as if it were already here in front of you." Susan noticed they
were becoming lost and had a thought which might improve
their concept of what she was saying.

She took out copies of the results of the greatest sales
campaigns in the history of the company. She gave both a
copy of the records and a blank sheet of paper. She remembered that on her last trip to the bank she had gotten some
fresh new dollar bills. She took them out of her purse and laid
them on the table.

"I want you to look at these figures, and get away from
each other and write down on the sheet of paper what you
personally want to do compared to what is on the record."
Each went to a separate section of the room, gazed at the
numbers and wrote down their expectations. When they came
back to Susan's desk, she handed them one of the new dollar
bills.

"Now, what we are about to do is apply everything we
have to make the goal you just wrote down become a reality.
I want you to look at the bill and imagine as many of them as
it takes to make the goal you wrote down." After a short pause,
in a slow voice, she continued, "Feel it all over. As you feel
this new bill notice the crackle of its newness. I want you to

place it to your ear and hear each sound it makes." They allowed her to be first and did as she did, with a slight smile on their faces.

"Now, smell it as you have now released the odor of the ink and paper." They did as she said. "Now, place it on your tongue and taste the bitterness, and remember the exhausting efforts of bitterness we overcame to get this job done."

As they each placed the bills in their mouth, the receptionist barged in without knocking, and all eyes met hers. It was obvious she knew she had interrupted a strange ritualistic conclave. As each person began to laugh aloud, she quickly bid her apologies and was gone. The laughter was just what was needed at the time. And they knew their ideas were bonded. Susan then asked for the written goals to be placed on her desk. It was really no surprise; each of the figures was double that of the best that was previously done.

"Then that's it! We have our goal amount. Now let's bust ass to get it done," Susan said, and they began to hold each other encircled as they knew what bonding had just happened to their futures together.

Looking back on those moments brought Susan a great deal of pleasure. It was then she found out the greatest meaning of what THE GIFT had to offer. It was simply because of the faith that was shared between the three believing souls, in group consciousness, bringing about the results that they had expected. There were problems that presented only momentary delays, but from that day in her office, they all were given a glimpse of what could be attained with collective belief. Reviewing what happened next all those many years ago, she knew why, or thought she knew why, she was in the position she held today.

It was the last days of the campaign and all day long they waited for the data from the accounting department which was never going to arrive. There was not a thought of anything else with Susan. After all, it would be both the end of one position in her life and the start of another. There was no doubt in her mind what the end results would be. It was just having it in black and white to show everyone that concerned her. Joe and Susan had worked hard together. They found each other's company most enjoyable. Though they had not experienced the kiss from her apartment again, there was an unspoken personal relationship. Susan had received several memos from him over the last weeks, and she wondered about an odd word that was handwritten, placed somewhere in the pages. 'OILY' was the word, and to save her soul she couldn't figure it out. At first she thought it was a technical reminder he placed there, but noticed it was on every one, without fail. Today, when the results came up from accounting, she would ask him what it meant. Just then her phone rang and it was Joe.

"They just sent me the results. You and Nancy should come down to my office as soon as possible," he spoke with a bit of hesitation in his voice and he hung up.

In a single bound, Susan was out the door and didn't take time to tell Nancy anything, just grabbed her by the hand and was off to Joe's office.

"Okay, knucklehead," Susan said, "let's see the results."

"Wait a second Susan, we... we're a half a million from the goal," Joe said handing her the report with a solemn stare.

Susan could hardly move the pages for the crowding of Nancy right next to her. Flipping through the technical data, there it was, on the fourth page. Joe's smile began to come first; he could not contain it any longer. He had said a half a million from the goal, but failed to mention, it was over the goal and not under. The entire plant could have heard the shouting from Joe's office. The simple approach had worked. Now, once again they would have to wait for the reaction of the firm and the plant. This would be a pleasure and it would take time. After all, crow when fixed just right took a little time to prepare.

That very night the trio had to take off for Shreveport, as it was closer than Little Rock, to do some serious celebrating. The sky was the limit and they found the nicest hotel, and taxied to eat and party at all the bars they could find. It didn't take Nancy long to have the usual flock of guys surround her. Soon after, she used the 'three's a crowd' excuse and assured them she would be fine and get a cab back to the motel and she left them. They were not all at ease with the idea, but rather than argue at the moment they agreed.

Alone now, and, since the alcohol had once again set both of them in a relaxed position, each now had the opportunity to express the pleasure which had been found at Susan's apartment. Then Susan remembered she was going to ask Joe about the word.

"Say big boy, I have a question for you" she said in her usual jovial manner. "Why did you always write OILY on your memos to me? Somewhere on every one I found it, sometimes I had to look pretty hard, but it was always there."

"Do you really want to know Susan? It's a kinda personal thing and I just wanted to see if you would notice," he came back, now making her want to know more than ever.

133

"Why yes. We aren't leaving here less you tell me."

Joe told her it was immature, but took a pen from his pocket and wrote O__ I L____ Y____ and showed Susan.

"So, what does it mean?" she said now with a bit more interest. Oh, I Love You were the letters he slowly filled in between the gaps. Susan's heart was taken back. For a moment she sat speechless.

"I'm sorry," he said. "You shouldn't have mentioned it," he quickly blurted.

"Damn it! There you go apologizing again. Why is it the first time we met you never apologized for hitting my car? Yet now every time you stand up for what you truly think, you say you're sorry?" She waited for him to answer.

"Well, the first time you were wrong in not looking back to see I was more than half way out of my parking space. And that was before I looked into your beautiful brown eyes and had the silly notion I could love you. Well there... I said it. I know, I might not have a chance with you, because...." and he stopped. Both of them sat staring at each other.

"Because what?" Susan blurted. "Because you are in a wheelchair? Because you are disabled? Because you are shorter than me? It makes no difference to me. It's what's in your heart that makes me care for you," and she stopped short realizing what she had just said. Joe heard it too.

"Well, I mean, you know, how I feel and all," her voice was now very flustered knowing what she had just revealed.

"No Susan, that's just it, I don't know how you feel, and

up to a minute ago you didn't know how I felt. Now what?" Joe said in a softer tone. "I cared for you from the Big W parking lot, and the kiss at your apartment will be one I will remember the rest of my life. But I have declined to show my feelings because of the push of this campaign, the office talk, and, yes my disability, even though it has been of a great deal of benefit in many ways. I have come to learn, because I can't offer the same physical features other men might, I have to offer those which are important to a woman most men simply take for granted. You would be pretty to me on your worst bad day. I would enjoy simply looking at you with the delight of knowing you were willing to share your life with me. My heart would be filled with gratitude to have the opportunity to be a part of your life, bad as well as good, and to be the one you wanted from your free choice. My first experience soured me with women, and, to be honest, I never wanted to open myself up to the pain of that hurt again. I know now much of the rejection I focused on was returning home without legs. Perhaps more than I should have. I'm not disabled; I am merely inconvenienced at times, unlike other men who take things for granted. I find myself compensating in ways that would offer a woman joy and pleasure," he said with a laugh. "I haven't made love in such a long time, maybe that is all in my mind too. "

He suddenly stopped talking and sighed. "Enough about it, most likely there are just a bit too many hormones running wild within me lately," and he reached for his beer.

Susan was touched as she listened to his low soft voice of truth. She remembered how this was what she wanted from Roy, which he never gave. She knew he had struck a nerve in her with his honesty, and it had been such a long time since anyone would have said she was pretty on her worst day. She was flattered. When he had spoken of the absence of making love, she remembered her own situation, and could relate to the hormone levels.

"Say Bubba, you ready to head back to the motel?" she asked smiling.

The smile growing on his face brought on an immediate "SURE", and it was not long till the cab had left them at Joe's motel room.

"You chicken to let a lady help you inside?" Susan said, already beginning to head for the door. "Give me your key," she said, but they were already in the air flying toward her. She unlocked the door and went inside, Joe followed. About half way into the room, she turned and for a moment just looked at him.

"I'll reserve my thoughts on love, after all, that's an awful long way down the road, but I will be honest and say you started a fire in me with your loving and caring words and, when you mentioned making love. Well...it's been a long time for me as well. I'd like to set the rules down up front, especially in matters of the heart, so here goes. We've had a few drinks and let's allow it to be the excuse, if an excuse is needed later. You are a very attractive man and I need you tonight. I may never need you again, and this is not intended to foster any further relationship, I'm not sure about you, as you may not be truly sure about me. Let's just accept each other for tonight, and let tomorrow start anew, agreed?"

Joe began to speak, "But what about...." and she stopped him,

"To agree or not to agree, that is the question Joe," she spoke firmly.

Without hesitation, he responded "Agreed."

She excused herself to his bathroom. She was surprised at the way all his toilet articles were neatly arranged. As she gazed at them the thought entered her mind about what she had just agreed to. This was a new experience for her. She had never made love to a disabled person. After all, how many people had? It was going to be a new experience and then she recalled his look back at the lounge. She shouted she would be a few minutes for she wanted to take a quick shower, he acknowledged her request. Soon she emerged from the bathroom wrapped in a motel towel designed for a midget. The room was dark. The light from the window was ample enough to allow her to see the room clearly. To her surprise, the room seemed neater than it had been when she left, something she was not accustomed to finding. Joe was on the right hand side of the bed. It had been such a long time for both of them.

She could feel the strange "stage fright" feeling, which quickly disappeared with the warm embrace of his arms around her.

Her feelings were not alone. Joe had pondered the question for those almost unending minutes while she was away. Not only the feeling of fright captured his mind, but doubt of his abilities to satisfy her. It had been a very long time for him too, and he almost began to shake with fear. Then he remembered that she had made things happen. She was confident in herself and instilled in him a confidence he had not known in years. His questions soon vanished when he took her in his arms and held her close. No longer would he allow doubt on what was yet to be or create disbelief in what he could do, and the apprehension was gone.

The movement of their bodies at first seemed awkward.

Positioning appeared to be a major concern with both of them. After the kiss, it was evident the concerns each had, just melted away. Like the first kiss of teenagers, it came with an expectation of joy. Slowly at first, barely touching their lips together, almost as if their touch would awaken them from the dream being shared. Gradually, with closed eyes, they began to experience what love was intended to be. Each one, wanting to give the other harbored emotions which were held captive for far too long. Seconds passed, and once again time stood still. Movements were so tender Susan barely felt Joe's touch as he shifted his body. As if blind, using his hands to see, he gently applied his fingertips to absorb every area he touched. As the kiss continued, she felt her senses start to generate feelings long missed as her inner tensions began to react. Their apprehension had vanished as he continued to explore her ever so compassionately, as if this was his first sexual encounter. His muscles, tuned to perfection from maneuvering without legs, allowed him to almost hover above her, as his response to the kiss became more intense. Soon his lips began to caress her cheeks, ears, and down her neck. The depth of his emotions were unlike anything Susan had ever felt. He seemed to know in advance of what her every thought might be and his vast arms gently moved her to position. Her allowance of his chivalry soon became more than either could withstand. With an almost unnoticed move of his arms, Susan was mounted on him as if perched upon a powerful stallion, and it was his turn to be at her mercy.

Perhaps it was the time between their last relationship, or the wonder of the moment, as each of them felt they were undergoing a phenomenon of the body and emotions they had never recalled. Before there was even a warning of climax, it was done. Breathing was quick and consuming, hearts rushed to the surge of passion, and although the room was extremely cool, shining beads glistened in the ray of light penetrating their space. No words were spoken to avoid risking the chance of the moment disappearing.

The inevitable cooling of their bodies quickly brought the sheet over them. In a single move, Susan's back was against Joe's chest as he held her in his arms. He slowly began to stroke her hair, savoring it as if it were neglected before. The effects of the combination of events of the evening quickly caused Susan to drift off to sleep, comforted in the security she felt. The exhaustion she had experienced did not allow her to open her eyes as he later moved away momentarily from her. Although still unable to move, she began to regain suitable consciousness when he returned. She heard him begin to speak. The tone of his voice was low and just barely a whisper as he spoke words he felt sure she would not hear.

"Sleep gently little one, for you know not the immeasurable pleasure of body and spirit you have given to me. I have long awaited this time, never having the courage needed to speak of my desires, and what was being set free from my captive heart. You have no knowledge of the love I have for you, for I myself have found it almost incomprehensible to think I could ever feel as I do. I have dreamed of you, just as you are, from the shell that holds your soul to the spirit that resides within. If you were awake I could not began to think, much less utter these words. The fear you would know my deepest feelings, and your rejection could ultimately cause my being to wither away. I have loved, and will continue to love you so," he ended as Susan began to turn.

As if synchronized, he rolled his back to her. He had just positioned his body to comfort when his ears heard, "I did hear every word. They were beautiful and there are three things I want to say. Thank you for your honest feelings; there is time to allow this to work; and good night." Joe drifted off to sleep, but it was not easy for Susan. His words had moved a part of her heart, which she had felt she had securely placed where it would not be found, but he did. He was not one to use words to his advantage, he hardly spoke unless spoken to, and those were the words of his heart.

The next few days at work were tense. No one mentioned a word about more than doubling the goal. Much to Susan's surprise, there were several calls at her desk from all forms of competition. First there were other advertising agencies, poultry plants, and several large companies who wanted her to contact them. She knew it had taken determination and the faith of the trio to make it work. How did so many other people find out? Why couldn't she get results from upstairs? She wondered. The reason soon became obvious. Her firm had long since taken credit for her work. From the moment the details of the sales results started to come in, Reynolds, Dunlap and Dyer had goaded the competition with "their" winning strategy, somehow omitting they had absolutely nothing to do with the smartest campaign in a decade. Susan began to return the calls. One by one it was obvious she was in demand. The offers were far more lucrative than what she had now, which was also no great surprise. The damned thing had worked, not only to produce revenue for everyone involved, but also to show her THE GIFT had fulfilled its promise. She realized as if all of a sudden it dawned on her, that she was exactly what she had wanted to be— a success. And then, her phone rang. Nancy was elated at the skinny she had picked up from a friend at the executive offices. The brass of the plant, along with the firm were giving her a dinner, and Mr. Dunlop himself would be calling today to extend his congratulations and tell her about the appreciation they were going to show for their efforts. Nancy, was always better at finding out secrets than the C.I.A., her excitement for Susan could not be hidden any longer. Susan had her call Joe into the office and it was a bit of a surprise what they were going to plan for the brass.

Such long remembering caused Susan to tire in her chair. It was almost five o'clock, so she got up and walked around to the bar and poured herself a, a drink she had made her favorite for years. A quick stretch and a grin, and she sat back to rejoin her most favorite memory of all. Carl Dunlop did call. She was his queen for the day and the firm was going to honor her with a dinner in the presence of the entire firm, the owners of the plant, media press and many more. It was her night; she was the belle of the ball. Susan had accomplished what no other person in the history of neither the firm nor the plant had ever done. It was her time to shine. When she came to the podium to speak, her words would again make history. She began first with words of gratitude for the adoration she had long sought, and stated she had to give thanks to others. She called Joe and Nancy forward.

"Upon coming to the plant, I found myself in an entirely hostile atmosphere. I was new, though unqualified for the job, and on top of which I was, and still am, a woman," she began.

"It was most obvious the road ahead was to be the roughest ride I was to take in my life. With all the southern charm the plant could offer, and the sneers my own company allowed, it was a total feeling of isolation I felt, until I met these two people. Nancy Pharr, who is not well known to most of you, is the very best one who could have been chosen to get whatever job she was assigned done with her maximum efforts. She possessed qualities I found not only amiable, but also rare. She gave of herself with honesty, dignity, caring and loyalty. I never once doubted she would be there to offer any and all support, which might have been needed. That feeling of support had to be present to do the task placed upon me, and was so often lacking when it was most needed from others. I am proud to not only call her my friend, but my partner. Thank you Nancy for this function and all accolades and respect are yours as they are mine." There was an uneasy hush around the room, as the presence of a surprise hovered like a cloud waiting for Susan to rain down upon them.

An extremely pleasant smile came upon Susan's face as she was looking at Joe.

"You all know Joe Butler. For years he has handled the most arduous task of dealing with both the plant and the firm, with wonderful results considering what he was forced to work with. Joe, like Nancy, was found to be a friend from the very start. He too was rich in qualities, which were freely given out of respect for the person I was, and loyalty for the person he recognized I could become. He has one more attribute, and only one over my feelings for Nancy. You see Joe has captured my heart, and we are going to consider making our partnership a bit more permanent."

The room gasped, and Joe, with his wide southern smile was among them, as she uttered the news.

"Joe, we have several things to discuss, but I want you, as well as these here tonight to know, like Nancy, you are responsible for, and deserve the credit for the success of the campaign." She gently kissed him as he and Nancy left the podium.

"And now for me!" she said, bracing herself with both hands, cleared her throat and allowed her piercing eyes to cut into the audience.

"It has been a challenge, to say the least, and I must confess somehow when the results of the campaign were released to others before me, I was shocked. The main reason shock was there was the competition came out of the woodwork to offer congratulations and employment opportunities, several of which were substantially better than my current position. They knew the results of the campaign before I did. Fear not, for of all the attributes I learned in this experience and the most important has been loyalty."

A sigh of relief could obviously be heard, as she continued.

"And yet, there are two more attributes which stand out clearer than the rest. Those of respect and confidence. One of the lessons I have learned is that in any relationship, the most needed commodities are those of respect and confidence. I found those with my two partners, when I failed to get them from those I had expected. I mentioned I had learned the value of loyalty. I say this because the lesson was a hard learned one, and because one must delve deeply inside one's soul and truly accept where loyalty must be adinfinitum to oneself and supporters. Because of the finding of true loyalty, I have chosen not to even consider offers to join your competition. Instead our trio has reached the mutual agreement and we will become everyone's competition and are forming our own agency. With the trade media present, it is the best opportunity to make this announcement, and convey a bit of advice, which will most likely fall on deaf ears. Never ever doubt the power of the individual, regardless of the newness, the ability or the gender, not to mention the power of faith that person may possess. When the positive power of faith is shared among friends, the combination I hope has proven to be awesome. It is with our sincere appreciation we accept your recognition of a job well done, and our hope the lessons learned from the past will be useful in the future. I have my doubts in this man's world, but the future is open and waiting for those who are open to welcome opportunity, and it may come in the most unusual of forms. Thank you. It has been an experience of a lifetime, and I will cherish the friends and relationships." She finished and the trio left the room, not to return again until Susan was chosen Woman of the Year.

The last ten years had passed so quickly she thought. Time just had a way of getting away. The phone had been kind to her by not ringing to interrupt her memories. Just then her secretary called to remind her of a dinner reservation. She had married Joe, shortly after they started the agency and Friday was a ritual for dinner. She was expecting him to come walking through the door.

Yes, expecting him to walk, not wheel. Joe had surprised them all, including himself. Susan's love had made him a whole man, and he wanted to look the part. It did not take much to be much taller than her, but his new legs reflected the feeling he had inside. When he walked up and put his arms around her, he wanted her to look up to him. He always knew and appreciated she had more drive and determination, yet he knew they were equal partners. Each gave just the right ingredient the other was missing. The being taller was a man thing. He had been much taller before the explosion, but was very satisfied to be able to stand level, eye to eye with her. When he was first fitted for his new legs he told her it would hurt his back to bend down so far, because she was so short and all, but she knew better.

Susan was all he had ever needed to convince him of the possibilities he possessed. He had never considered a prosthesis until she made him believe in himself. Although she had never shared THE GIFT with him, he gleaned from her all he needed to gather his will together and change for her.

She and he had found it is the love inside one's self that makes the outer person. Each one was independent and it was the caring for the real person inside that caused the love to grow and flourish. She had wondered if he was the one intended to receive THE GIFT, yet somehow knew he had no need, as he already had the peace and satisfaction inside, all he needed was her. She wondered though, it had been so long, was there someone who it was intended or was it a special prize for her alone. Just then Nicole surprised her with a visit. Nicole had taken a job in Atlanta, married and was on her way to what she thought was her dreams. She was not the same Nikkie, although this was not strange. Susan had become so involved with work over the years the closeness between mother and daughter somehow had disappeared. As most mothers and daughters tend to disagree about life, Nicole had taken her own road and was her own woman, but the mother in Susan saw an all to familiar view, and thought of herself so many years ago. Without a word, Susan knew something was wrong, and she saw the look in Nicole's eyes that told her she was unhappy. Could it be her own daughter was to be the one to now benefit from THE GIFT? It was only a matter of time till the answer was revealed.

THE HOMECOMING

Nicole tried to act like her same old self, as she walked unannounced into her mother's office, but she was in front of the wrong person to try that trick. Susan recognized the facade, as any mother would. Nicole had something complicated on her mind and her heart that was eating away at her. She was never one to hide it well. Joe, her step father, was there. She had really never seen eye to eye with him and this was fine with her. It was her mother's choice and her approval or disapproval was not important. He had recognized the distance and disrespect Nicole had always had for her mother, and had never fully accepted the fact. No other words had to be spoken between a mother and daughter, each knew a time would come later when they would reach each other. Now was not the time at the Friday ritual dinner.

The meal was the best Nicole had remembered for a while. The conversation seemed to skirt around any issues that anyone thought might be sensitive, and all went well. They drove home to their North Little Rock house and Joe excused himself to allow them to visit. He always knew when to leave them alone. Susan walked over to the bar and said, "Well, Nikkie, I guess you have something on your mind and a drink might calm us both down. What will you have?"

"Mother, how can you always tell when I have a problem? You always know when something is wrong! I'll have a

Seven and Seven."

"Nikkie, you are twenty eight years old, I'm your mother, it comes with great instinct to know when you have a problem. Besides you're wearing it all over you. Now, here's your drink, come clean and let's not play games about honesty, okay?" She sat in one of the coffee table chairs and waited for Nicole to sit in the other.

"There could be a thousand things wrong, your marriage, your job, your life in general and there is no use in playing twenty questions. You have known for some time now I don't scold, blame, or offer my opinions about your life, unless of course, you ask. You and I both know I stopped that a long time ago." Susan stopped talking, and turned the conversation over to Nicole.

"It's my marriage, the job and yes, my life in general. Taylor and I have reached the end of a five-year battle. It's time to go our own way. I can't blame him for everything. I'm as stubborn as he is. The first year was fun, but neither one of us was ready to marry. I'm not sure if we ever truly loved each other as much as the idea of being in love itself."

"Oh, I see!" said Susan. "And have you reached any legal decisions? Do you know for sure that it's over? Is that why you are here?" she asked, prompting the conversation back to Nicole.

"Yes, the papers were served today and I didn't want to stay in Atlanta alone. I screwed up the start of this relationship. I wanted to finish it right, without discussion. But, I, I quit my job too, and the fact is, I want to come home for a while and settle my thoughts. Right now my thinking process is a bit confused." Nicole said with some crow between the teeth.

"It's all right Nikkie, you are welcome to stay for as long as you need. It might even be a good time for us to get to know each other again. I'll call Brad and he and Betsy can come down for a weekend," Susan said hoping to cheer her up.

"If it's all the same with you mother, I'd just as soon share my time with you alone right now, maybe later Brad can come down. I have always butted into his business and he told me long ago my relationship with Taylor would never work. My pride needs a bit of mending before I take on his smartassed comments, if you know what I mean."

"Sure, I realize you and Brad were never really that close. You just let me know when you feel like a bit more company. In the meantime, you might consider coming to work for me; I can always use your help. Not suggesting right away, but something you may consider."

"Thanks, mom, but I don't think in the state of mind I am currently in I'd be much help to you, me or anyone. I need to sit back and take an assessment of my life. What do I want, where I am going? How I am going to get there? And can I ever truly fall in love? All are things now going through my mind. The lust is great, enjoy the hell out of that, yet I'm not satisfied. By the time someone is my age they should have a husband, a career, children, the whole damned nine yards, and I don't," was her frustrated reply.

"Well, my lovely child, you are finding it out a great deal sooner than I did. I too thought I loved Roy. Then the real world engulfed us, with kids, bills to pay, dreams we wanted, yet never really totally shared, and when we parted I was also very confused. But, maybe there's hope; maybe it's not as bad as the picture you have painted. Yes, you do need time to think, to go within yourself and see just what is there. I might be able to help," she said as she thought again, maybe it was Nicole who was to get THE GIFT. Yet the next words that came out of Nicole's mouth gave her questions.

"Mom, I appreciate your positive thinking, the things you have done with your life, but I've got to find my own way. I need your support now, not your it worked for me, it can work for you ideas. I just don't want it, don't need it, can't take it now." The conversation faded to other more pleasant subjects, though the thoughts of the moment remained deep in their minds.

Susan remembered how she thought back when she was Nicole's age and how much patience she had learned over the last ten years. There would be more tomorrow's, more time to have opportunities to see if Nicole was the one to have THE GIFT. After all, she had been promised it would be taken care of, yet the mother in her wanted to reach out to Nicole, and try and make things easier for her.

Susan, being much older and wiser now, knew not to pressure Nicole. For several weeks there was just rest and relaxation. As with most people, with nothing to do, the signs of boredom began to appear. At her mother's request, Nicole went to the office and gave a hand in the departments that had rush jobs. She avoided the production department, as that was Joe's pride and joy. She was not running the risk of offending him in the least. It might have been her situation or just her attitude, but she was not getting into that line of work. She may have felt uneasy because the area was what her mother had complained about most when Nicole was a child. Nonetheless, try as hard as she thought she could, there was no excitement. What was she going to do?

Susan recognized Nicole was having a problem with fitting in with the business. One day she took her out to a long lunch. Today was the day she thought she might tell her about THE GIFT. It was not to be the best of days for communication for them. After eating an enormous amount, because of the tension between them, Nicole said bluntly to her mother, " Mother, what do you have on your mind? Something has been eating at you, so just tell me."

"Nicole, I have noticed you are unhappy with yourself, your situation, and with the company. I think I might be able to help, but you need some idea of what it is you truly might enjoy. Think, right now, what is it that you enjoy? Right off the top of your head."

"Okay, now don't laugh, I enjoy eating, but differently than other people. It's the arrangement or the design of the food. Like an artist's creation.... Just like the meal we just ate; a creation that is appealing to the eye and the taste of the mind's expectation. Do you know what I mean?" she said with doubt of the reply.

"Yes, you mean you enjoy the creativity of the plate, as well as the food prepared, the lay out, so to speak. That, I can totally understand, it's been my business for years, I had no idea you were inclined to think that way." Susan said with a sparkle in her eye. Maybe Nicole now at last had shared something they could communicate about. " Well, you know we have several food manufactures that we design ads for. Haven't you been working with some of the many people in those departments that have those responsibilities?" Susan inquired.

"No, mother, I stayed away from such. I have been doing

the business crap and working with the assholes of your business. Exactly why it all seemed so very boring to me. You know I studied art in college, and to be honest, for the last few years, I have been drawn back to it. To do the thing I had enjoyed. Taylor and my job have held me captive from doing the thing I truly wanted to do, ART. Food in its proper place is art to me." With a laugh and another sip of wine she giggled.

Susan felt much better about discovering this side of Nicole, which she had never really taken the time to discover. Perhaps, THE GIFT could wait after all. It had waited for years now anyway.

"Wait... I have a great idea. I have a new campaign coming up for one of our toughest of clients. The soup companies, the big "C". This might need just a bit of your imagination. After all, how long can one really come up with ideas to glamorize soup?"

This was Susan's opportunity to give Nicole a test, and see what she really could do. Besides, she always welcomed a new idea, and it might be just the touch she needed with Nicole. THE GIFT was quickly forgotten, and Susan saw another opportunity to get to know Nicole much better. Perhaps her thoughts were very much premature.

THE OWNER

His gait was extremely fast and his eyes were quick to notice anything out of place. This was his latest store opening and he was more observant than he might otherwise have been, too much was at stake. This was his twenty-seventh store. He had not been wrong in the demographics before, but he surrounded himself with knowledgeable people. Nicholas Andrews was a complicated man. He was quiet and his thoughts were calculating, not shared with anyone, especially his private ones.

His business associates were never able to get close to him. He was not like other men. There was almost a bitterness inside which slightly permeated his demeanor, both business and personal. He was very well off considering he was an uneducated man. Meaning, he was not a college graduate. He had attended one of the finer schools, yet his behavior had threatened his expulsion prior to his voluntary leaving. It was his young opinion that knowledge he had to acquire in the business world, was not something that could be learned in schools. He felt that he would be better off to get his education the hard way. From a very young age, Nicholas had worked in grocery stores as a bag boy at first, to assistant manager later. It took several jobs for him to finally find a manager that both took him, and his attitude, under his wing. Mr. Sparks was that kind of a man, Nicholas was comfortable being guided. Sparks was retired military and ran the base commissary. He represented both a manager of the operation and a leader of men. Each of the attributes would be a commodity Nicholas knew he would have to master. At last, Nicholas started to hide some of his outward ways. He took the cotton out of his ears and put it in his mouth and absorbed everything he could. He knew one day he would own a chain of grocery stores, and there was nothing stopping him once his mind had been set.

Nicholas Andrews was a handsome man. He had never gotten married, a surprise to many, but marriage to him would risk sharing parts of himself; the ones he kept hidden. He never mentioned his family, where he was raised, or what social level he enjoyed. In his position, being social was important, but not one of the things he enjoyed. His blue eyes seemed to make most people very uncomfortable if he stared too long. He seldom smiled, which could have been a good reason for their uneasiness. There was however a warm gentle kindness that showed at the proper times, and he never was a selfish person. He knew all of his employees and they all knew him. He had his way of finding out things. If there was a situation, whether with a long standing employee or a new one, he always knew about it. If he felt loyalty from the employee, the condition was quickly remedied. Although it may have been known where the final help came from, it was never admitted by Nicholas nor was it rumored by employees. The opposite was true if disloyalty was sensed.

"The store looks fine," Nicholas said to the new manager. "There are a few problems I have noted and will have dictated and delivered to you tomorrow for correction, but overall it looks damn good," he continued. "Oh yes, there was one thing and I know you know better. At the end of aisle three, you have a display of the large canned pineapple juice that is too damn high. There are pictures around the center, which could cause people to take from the bottom. See about it first thing," he snapped. The snapping was common for a new store opening, and regretfully the new manager would never remember the display.

"Yes Sir, I'll have someone get right on it," was his reply and his mind was back to other things being said.

The new manager had heard rumors about the picky ways Mr. Andrews had with a new store opening. There's only one chance for a first impression, and Nicholas was not going to waste it because of employees who might overlook the slightest detail a customer would find. He had found in youth, if something was going to be done to his satisfaction, he would have to do it to begin with. Nicholas was rushing to prepare for a dinner party. His quick answers and manners indicated his impatience. He always hated to have to attend those parties.

North Little Rock was an average size suburb of Little Rock, but was much more influential than average. Going to social functions was not something Nicholas Andrews cared for at all. It was a necessary evil and a very important part of his business. He had to kiss a lot of butts, and the best and most important ones for getting things done his way, were always at these functions. He always knew every person there, and if he didn't, the hostess quickly remedied it. He walked into the black tie affair and within minutes found those with whom he was not acquainted. This time it was a very attractive woman who caught his attention almost immediately. Without hesitation he found the hostess and inquired about her.

"Bethany, what a lovely gathering, as usual you have outdone yourself. How do you find the time to plan such elegant events?" were his first remarks.

"Nicholas, you silver tongued devil, your flattery is always welcomed. Just who are you wondering about tonight?" she asked. The direction of his eyes pointed to the young lady in the dark teal dress and his words were not necessary.

"Oh, I see. Yes, that is a new one for you, and might I add congratulations on your very good taste. She is the daughter of Susan Bagwell. Nicole is her name. I'm sorry I can't recall her last name just now. Would you like me to introduce you to her?" With a quick nod, they were on their way toward her. Nicole was just ending a conversation and as she turned, accidentally walked right into Nicholas' arms.

"Nicole, darling, I want to introduce you to the man you almost fell over. This is Nicholas Andrews. One of our more distinctive businessmen, and I might add, he's unmarried too. Oh, there's Lucy Ethridge. I've got to speak with her. Please excuse me," and she was gone.

In all the noise of a party of this size, there was a strange quiet each of them felt. The glance they shared was quick, yet deep. An uncomfortable feeling seemed to fall on them for no apparent reason.

"I'm not really falling for men these days, but you're obviously an exception. Please excuse me." A smile that had started when their eyes met was starting to grow. It was contagious, and he spoke with his mouth starting his own smile.

"That's all right, I should not have been so close, didn't mean to invade your personal space. So you are Susan Bagwell's daughter I am told," was Nicholas' response.

"Yes, you already have one on me, and who's son are you?" she asked.

Instantaneously his smile was gone, and she felt the distance immediately begin to form. Nicole had a quick wit about her and noticed the change. "I'm sorry, your father beat you or something?" was her come back. She thought how quick she always was with a snide remark. This time she felt she had been a little too quick. His eyes told her it was not appreciated. She wanted to take it back, but it was too late. She would simply have to deal with that mistake and try and watch it in the future.

"No, my father left us when I was a teenager. I never saw him again. Let's talk about something else, if you don't mind. I don't know Susan personally, although her firm has done some of our ads. Do you work for her?" he said hoping the subject of family would vanish. Although he had secrets, his eyes revealed his intentions and Nicole knew the time had come for the subject to change.

"No, not with anyone at present. I have considered a position in her company, with food displays of all things," she said.

"Great, then maybe I can get more bang for my bucks. You see I own several food stores in town and in our business a picture truly is worth more than a thousand words," he stopped and looked closer at her. "Have we met before? Although you don't look familiar, I have this uncanny feeling we have met somewhere before."

"You do need help. That line is way out of date. Unless you have lived in Atlanta or outside of Chapel Hill, North Carolina, where I went to school, the possibility is rare," she answered. Damn, she caught herself doing it again, but this time she knew she was playing hard to get and quickly gave herself a good excuse.

"No, seriously I get the feeling I have known you before. I don't usually have those sorts of feelings, but it's a nice one I assure you," he spoke lower and continued to watch for her expression.

"Well, I truly don't think so, Mother was not feeling well, had a headache, and asked me to attend. I haven't been here very long and she thought getting out, with the lure of business, might help. I'm new to this area and have no idea of who all these people are, or how I might benefit from being here," Nicole said in a bored manner.

"Well, I might be of assistance as I know most of them. See the man over there by the fireplace with the wine glass in his hand. That's the Governor, Dale Bumpers, and next to him is his esteemed assistant. Most of the people here are either politicians, lawyers, or very powerful business persons, male and female. Oh, see the couple coming in from the patio, over there? That's an up and coming politician. Let's see, his name is Bill and her name is, oh, what is it? Hillary, yes Hillary and Bill Clinton. Talk is they are going to be big players in the Democratic party. I don't know if he will make it big or not. I doubt it, no one from Arkansas could ever get to the White House which is what I hear is his ultimate goal. Come, I'll introduce you to several people in the room and you can tell your mother the party was not a total wash," he said taking her arm and staying very close.

They spent the rest of the evening together. For Nicholas it was a very welcomed change. Nicole also enjoyed spending the evening with a handsome man with potential. Each of them had drawn a barrier line around their heart, so the conversation was one of pleasant subjects. Cautiously staying away from any topics that could be misunderstood. There was obviously an attraction there.

Each of them would allow time for it to take its course. They both thought there would be enough time to deliberate matters of the heart. This was not the last time they would meet, and they knew it.

Many thoughts surged through the mind of Nicholas Andrews on his ride home that night. He was one to fall asleep thinking about things which needed to be done the next day, yet this night was different. As he drove he found a bit of her perfume on his coat sleeve, which brought a smile. He brushed his hand through his hair and laughed. He figured it was a nice meeting, someone that had caused his mind to consider distant possibilities, but not anything serious he had to worry about. His last thoughts were of her face as he closed his eyes to sleep.

I made a good impression, she thought. Good for the business and mother would be pleased at meeting the decision maker of a large grocery chain. It was a great excuse for the way she acknowledged the happiness she felt in her heart. It was not good enough to fool her own feelings. She laughed at herself for noticing the way he leaned against the wall, the way he wore his tie, and how his cologne was vague and just noticeable. She was hoping that her mother was going to be up waiting for her; she wanted to tell her all about him. That would have to wait, but the vision was not so easily erased from her thoughts. As the light on the nightstand was turned out, she wished his memory were so easy.

THE CONFRONTATION

It was all very evident. Nicole had enjoyed herself at the function. Her constant discussion of Nicholas Andrews made it apparent. A week or more had passed and she did not seem to be getting into the company as much as Susan thought she might have. The old Nicole was returning, and Susan was hoping to see some change in her by now. She had fallen back into the slump, not wanting to go to the office. She seemed to have lost her interest in food design, for whatever reason. Susan felt it was time to take matters into her own hands, again. She waited for just the right moment. Then one night when Joe was out of town, and she and Nicole had returned from dinner Susan decided it was time. She had practiced the conversation a thousand times in her head. She was finally going to tell her about THE GIFT. She just knew Nicole was the one meant to receive what she had long wanted to give to her.

"Let's sit down and talk, Nicole, woman to woman," Susan uttered in her usual way.

It might have set Nicole on the defensive as she was really in no mood to get into any deep lengthy discussions with her mother. She knew what was going on inside her own mind. Nicole was indeed spoiled, but it was self-taught. Unlike her mother, she had independence from a very young age and nothing was going to get in the way of what she wanted; including and certainly not limited to men, jobs and whatever else might be thrown her way. Headstrong was not the proper word; stubborn came close, and selfish fit in somewhere. She liked to think of herself as a simple woman. She only wanted one thing in life, her way.

"Mother, I'm not really ready to get into what I fear is a debate about my life situation now," was her comeback. She walked over to the bar and poured herself a stiff drink knowing any excuse she could conjure would not stop the inevitable.

"What I want to discuss is not about your life now, or the circumstances you just happen to be in at the moment. It's more about your future."

Nicole immediately started getting herself ready to let the battle begin. She appreciated, in small measure, what her mother had done for her these last few weeks, but she was not ready to make any serious decision about anything. Taylor was her last decision and she was still not sure she had made the right one. However, she was not the type of person to go back on anything she had already decided upon.

"Mother, I appreciate your letting me hang here. I needed the respite, as you know, but we have grown so far apart these last few years, to be honest and without offense, you don't know shit about my life, who I really am or what I want. I know you mean well, and your intentions are honorable, but I'm just not in the mood for a long lecture tonight."

Well, Susan was taken aback by the fact Nicole was now showing much more of her independence. The truth was, and had been for some time, she was right. Susan had changed the person she once had been and was enjoying her new found self. She did not feel guilty about not paying attention to the wants and desires of her children. She had given them the best years of her life. It was not a matter of love, she loved Nicole and Brad, but their life was for them to walk, as was hers and she felt it was time they made decisions. Yet, she felt extremely drawn to Nicole. At last she was starting to be honest with her feelings. This was a good sign to her and she felt even more secure it was time to tell her about THE GIFT.

"Nicole, I'm not going to lecture you on your life, one way or the other. You seem to forget I am not only your mother, but also I am an individual myself. I have lived, learned and loved, all on my own, and it is this I want to discuss with you. I want to tell you something. All I want to know right now is, are you willing to listen seriously to what I have to say?" Susan said and waited for Nicole to respond.

Nicole knew when her mother had that tone of voice; it was no use trying to avoid the situation. It was much easier to accept the fact that what was going to be said, was going to be said, like it or not. Nicole fixed a drink at the beginning of this conversation.

"Okay, lets get this started. Sounds like this is going to be a long conversation designed to give me guidance through my troubled waters." Nicole replied. Her mother was not excused from her snide remarks.

"Not really, it's a confession as much as it is a guidance. I have not told a soul what I am about to tell you," and Nicole's ears perked up right away.

Her demeanor changed quickly. There had always been a drive in her mind to be better than her mother. In Nicole's eyes she had failed at that goal. Now she might be privileged to know a shortcoming, maybe it would lessen the distance between her and her mother. Susan continued. "As a mother, I never wanted to show any of my faults, God knows I had enough you and Brad knew about. This hidden fault was never brought out during your adolescent years. It was hard enough just trying to keep peace with Roy, a job and the responsibilities that went along with a home. What I have to say, I think you may, or may not understand. You took the divorce fairly well. Your father admitting to an affair and put all the guilt on him. Perhaps it was the ease in the way the divorce proceeded which hid the emotional battles we were both going through at the time."

Susan sipped her and waited to see the reaction on Nicole's face. There was none, and no words came fourth either, just a blank look waiting for more information from her mother.

"Roy, had been carrying on the affair for sometime. Things had gotten cold, routine or just downright boring in our marriage. I was just as much at fault as he was. For years I realized we were just playing the daily parts of a marriage." With concern in her eyes as to how Nikkie was going to react, she cautiously said, "One day, I met a man, quite by accident, and I had a one day affair." Susan stopped and noticed the change in Nicole's eyes as she revealed her secret.

"I won't try to justify it. There is really no way to explain what happened or the eventfulness of that day, but there was never another meeting. It was not because I would not have. I never have been totally sure. The fact is, he committed suicide after our day together and there was a great deal of guilt on my part, for that as well as the dishonor I had caused my family and myself. The facts are, before I could digest all that had happened, your father asked for a divorce. I was confused and bearing what I just told you, it was the only course of action which seemed reasonable," Susan said in a lower apologetic sound. It was not difficult to the see the thoughts churning in Nicole's mind. Her facial expression quickly gave Susan notice that there was a much more serious sneer as she prepared to speak. Her posture almost made Susan regret she had told her. Nicole was like a snake about to strike.

"You mean you let Daddy take all the blame for the failure of the marriage? You let us believe he was the sinful one, while you, all the time had been just as guilty of the same transgression?" Nicole fired back.

"We were not children mother. We needed to know the marriage was falling apart, and that you were equally as responsible as Daddy was. All these years Brad has held that against him, yet never said anything to you for fear of only rubbing salt into an old wound. I myself have tried, with fear of every imperfection of mine. I would disappoint you. You see your perfect world of what things should be, rather than how they damned well were," Nicole said in disappointment.

"So now, I'll take the blame and the delayed punishment for not being totally honest. I could have kept silent, but I wanted you to know. It was something that came out of the affair that changed my life and I truly think you are the one I was meant to pass it on to. I have grown to believe in the doctrine it contains. If you practice its principles, you'll reap the rewards it promises. You see everything which has happened to me over the last ten years has been directly because of what I learned back then. Everything I ever wanted has come about, and now you can also have that. I want you to have THE GIFT," she said expecting Nicole to be excited with the prospects of her offering.

"How could you think that I could, or even would accept

anything from an affair? I can't believe you think I could use an instrument of destruction of our home to help me mold my life! It may have been justified to you, but I can't and won't accept it!" Nicole saw she was becoming over emotional, and wanted to calm things down. Perhaps she was viewing her mother as more than mortal human. She thought of the times her mother had been treated badly by her father and deserved the attention he so often overlooked.

"Okay, perhaps I was too hard with those statements, even a bit unfair in as much as you were belatedly being honest. It was all such a shock and I reacted from my own personal rejection of what impact it had on me. Mother, I love you, and I wish you could have trusted me, and confided in me. At this point, I'm not ready for any thing of this nature. I see the potential to be my own person in food design, maybe have my first opportunity with Nicholas Andrews' company. The doors are starting to open, and, to be completely honest with you, I'm not ready emotionally or intellectually for reminders of your past actions. Let's just take this a bit slower, one step at a time. I will accept your assistance with food design, with gratitude. It's a start anyway Mother," Nicole's comments were accepted, Susan knew she had been wrong about the past. However, she felt equally sure Nicole was the one intended to have THE GIFT.

The next few weeks were truly a delight at work for Nicole. She was changing again to her old self. It might have been the almost immediate success of the food design idea she had, or perhaps it was the prospects of working eventually with Nicholas Andrews. At any rate, the progress was phenomenal. She had spent a great deal of time with label photography. She learned it was the tricks of the trade which made the picture look good, not the food itself. The surprises that she learned made her loose her appetite on more than one occasion. The pictures were made to look much more appealing by the light images the camera captured, enhancing the taste buds with fake colors that had to be added to almost every shot.

Considering everything as a whole, Nicole was making herself quite at home with the company, much to Susan's surprise. She remembered how THE GIFT was introduced to her. She decided to apply the same technique to Nicole. This would give her an opportunity to reject it on her own. Nicole's reaction would be private, and not having it forced down her throat, would be an advantage for Susan. She had to be out of town, and would place it in Nicole's purse, just like she received it. The morning of her leaving, a strange twist of fate occurred. Nicole had decided she had absorbed all she could from the company, it's departments, labs, technicians, and the like. It was time she went out into the field and see what the competition was doing. She knew Nicholas would be in town at his new store. The grand opening was just about to take place, and she could use it as a good excuse to see him again. What she did not know, was Susan had placed THE GIFT in her purse so it could be found while she was away. She felt comfortable with the thought they could discuss this matter when she returned later in the week.

As Nicole was on her way to the store her only thoughts were about Nicholas. She could never remember a time when she felt so comfortable with someone in such a short time. Realizing they had only met once, she could not understand why she could not get him out of her mind. When she was at work and she got a new idea, or thought of something funny, he was the first person to come to mind that she wanted to share these things with.

They had talked on the phone quite often since the first

encounter at the party. They were getting to know each other a little better, but the barrier was still up guarding their inner feelings and dreams. Nicole often wondered what drove Nic to be the person he was today. It was still a mystery, as to why they felt so compelled to be close to each other. It was rare to last over a day or two when they did not feel the need to reach out and talk. It was like they were two halves of a whole when they came together. Now they were going to be face to face again, and Nicole was a little nervous. Would they be as comfortable with each other in person as they seemed to be on the phone? These and other questions would be answered in just a few hours. She hoped the answers were what she wished for but yet, right now, she herself was not sure what they were. She was glad, however, to have had the confrontation with her mother. Somehow it justified these impetuous feelings for a man she could be falling in love with, or did she simply just need a soft place to fall at this point in her life?

THE NEW GROCERY

Nicholas assumed his commands would always be carried out. Never had anyone failed to do anything he had instructed, until now. The day was perfect for a GRAND OPENING and the crowd was already coming early into the store. He was late in arriving and didn't make his usual final walk through. Excitement was in the air, there was always a side bet with the other managers of what problems they would encounter on the first day. No one could have predicted what disaster awaited.

As Nicholas sat at the desk in the manager's office his mind began to wander. Such strange occurrences had been happening to him a lot over the last few weeks. This was very foreign for him, as he was a very focused individual. The subject he kept thinking about was always the same, Nicole. He didn't understand this. No woman had ever affected him like this. He often tried to understand what this meant because he was a very logical and by the book kind of man. He would sit and wonder what she was doing, what she was thinking, all the way to what she was wearing. Usually when he got to this point his mind would bring him back to the present. He just did not understand what kind of pull this woman had on him. He kept trying to reject it, but it was always there, in the back of his mind. He never thought much about a future that included a woman. That in itself, scared him to death.

Nicole had seen her mother off at the airport and decided today was the day to visit Nicholas' new store. She knew several of the vendors had used this opening to introduce new products, and she was going to check out the competition. The parking lot was packed. Free hot dogs and a southern soda brought everyone out. The surprise was how early people could eat them, hot dogs and a southern did not appeal to Nicole for breakfast. The key word must have been free.

As she entered the store, a kid was running wild. He appeared to be too old to be giving his mother these types of problems. He was shouting, running plus several other irritating actions. Nothing in Nicole's mind, that a quick spanking could not remedy. She was never so glad to have the brat leave. She then went to find Nicholas. He was in the office, at the manager's desk and by the smile on his face, knew Nicole's voice the instant she spoke. His smile told her immediately of his genuine gratitude at her presence.

"Nicole, what brings you here on Hell Day? I am truly flattered!" he said with a huge grin. "There are so many distractions during these first hours, I regret I will not be able to give you the personal attention I would like to."

"Why Nicholas Andrews, you vain rascal. What makes you think I came to see you?" she asked with her soft teasing smile. "But I'm glad I could make a legitimate excuse to see you again, I did enjoy our first meeting so," she said anxiously awaiting his reply.

"I...I was trying to arrange for us to have some time together again, I promise. This grand opening, not to mention the other stores, has taken up far too much of my time I would much rather have been spending with you," he said and she smiled. "So, what is your excuse anyway?" he asked, figuring her interest now they were face to face.

"I told you, I'm seriously into food design. I know there are several new products being introduced here, and I wanted to see what my competition was doing. After all, I want your business for the store brands you carry," she said with a grander smile.

"You picked a hell of a day to come, the crowds are outrageous, but of course it's good for me. Rings the cash registers," he said as he found himself looking deeply at her gorgeous face.

"I don't mind the crowds. It's these unsupervised kids the mothers let run wild, which give me fits. Besides I thought you might need a break soon and take me out for coffee," she said with a sparkle in her eyes.

"Hey, that's a grand idea, I would love to. You go do what you want to do and I'll take care of a few things here. When you're done come back and we'll take in the coffee shop down the street. Heard it's wonderful!" came his reply and they parted.

Nicole was so overtaken by the designs and layouts she had to go back and get a cart. Some of the pictures were great and she was going to study how to improve on them. She was determined to get Nicholas' business on her own. The aisles were wider than most, a new tradition in mega marts, but the vast amounts of people still made them tight. She had just reached the end of the third aisle when he came from nowhere, screaming like an animal and pushing his mother's cart with incredible speed. It was obvious he didn't see her, or for that matter, even cared if she was there. The sound could be heard throughout the entire store as the cans came crashing down. The kid hit Nicole's cart so hard she was forced into the display Nicholas had told the manager to rearrange.

He knew immediately, from his sixth sense, what had happened. The screams from the back of the store brought him to his feet at once. There was a sickening feeling that came over him suddenly. Never hitting the steps down from the office, Nicholas bounded with lightning speed to the location of the doomed display. There he found her, unconscious and bleeding from the head. Nicole lay covered with large heavy cans.

"My God, Nicole!" he cried and began moving the cans from around her. He grabbed the nearest store pager from a support beam and shouted at the top of his voice,

"Call 9-1-1 NOW!" he shouted.

His voice carried the message throughout the store. Every employee had heard that tone before and instantly knew whatever it was, it was serious, yet there was something else there they did not recognize from him, panic. He had never allowed himself to reveal that emotion before.

Although she looked dead, he found a pulse and ordered everyone to stand back. He insisted several people start picking up the cans and clear the aisle for the paramedics. He tried to get her to wake up by shouting her name,

"Nicole! Nicole! Can you hear me?" There was no response. There was no movement.

He had never known such fear before. As he looked down at the blood that ran from the side of her head he knew the feelings he had were much more than he wanted to admit. In any smaller situation, which this one was a large one, he would have immediately considered the ramifications of a lawsuit, this time it never crossed his mind. He only wanted to hear her voice again.

The ambulance arrived quickly. As they were taking Nicole out the door, Nicholas looked at the manager. As they say, if looks could kill, the manager would have been on a stretcher too. He had been told to change the display and knew right away Nicholas's thoughts.

"No time to discuss this now, I'm going to the hospital with her. This matter is far from over and you know it. I don't know when I'll be back, but this place is in your hands now and you damn well better check and recheck. This can't, and won't, happen again," he said with fire in his eyes.

His car was just behind the ambulance and he had driven like a maniac to catch them. Nicole was just being taken out of the ambulance as he ran to her side and through the double emergency room doors holding her hand along the way. At the nurse's station he caught someone's attention and " This is Nicole," and he stopped. "Hell, I don't even know her last name, but that's not important. I'm Nicholas Andrews and she was hurt at my store. I want the very best you can give her. Cost is no object. If you need more doctors, just tell me, and you'll have them." He spoke with a genuine worried tone.

"I understand, please just go over there and have a seat in the waiting room."

"Did anyone bring her purse, so we can get identification?" the nurse asked.

Not responding, he ran out to the ambulance and there it

was in the front corner of the ambulance. He grabbed it, and within seconds handed it to the charge nurse, then walked to the small waiting room. It seemed like days were passing, and not a word. He knew constant asking would do him no good and only annoy the nurses. Finally a nurse came out. He tried desperately to figure out Nicole's condition from the expression on her face, and was relieved when she smiled softly.

"Mr. Andrews, the doctors have found Ms. Garrison has a severe concussion and will remain unconscious for an undetermined time. She has no broken bones, but is bruised badly and will be awfully sore for several days. It was not felt she needed intensive care, but we are placing her in a private room. You mentioned additional staff? If you like we can have a private duty nurse available to her on a twenty-four hour basis for these next few days," she said as she watched his reaction.

"Garrison, I never even knew her last name." he mumbled. "Yes, I would like it very much. Can I go see her now?" he questioned.

"Not right away. She is being admitted and is on some pretty strong medications. However, as soon as she is taken to her room you can visit as long as you like. When one suffers a concussion it is better to have someone talking to them, just to assure them they are not alone. Might help bring her out of it."

He got the assigned room number and was there when she arrived. After the nurses finished and left, he just stood by her bedside. He thought how helpless she looked and how it was his fault. Regardless of his orders, he felt ultimately responsible this had happened. It could have happened to someone else, but it didn't. It happened to Nicole and brought an agonizing sorrow to his heart. His hard core interior was beginning to break down. He had never looked at a woman the way he looked at Nicole, and now, the joy in his thoughts of her was just offsetting the regret. Just then her eyelids moved. He was watching for the slightest motion, and he took her hand.

"Nicole, it's me Nic! Can you hear me" but again there was no response.

He was there the rest of the day and long into the night. He talked to her about everything and nothing, hoping she would respond. His five o'clock shadow changed his business appearance into a rather rugged blue collar worker, but he was still very handsome. An orderly knocked on the door and came in with her clothes and her purse, which had been left in the emergency room.

"Here ya go, sir. I brought your wife's stuff," he said and laid them down on the bedside table.

"Thank you," Nicholas said and started to pick them up to put them in the closet. The purse slipped from his grip and hit the floor spilling most of its contents.

He felt awkward even handling a woman's purse, but began to pick up the contents and replace them. One envelope didn't seem to want to go back in properly. He became interested in its very old appearance. It was opened; he had nothing to do. He figured if it was personal, he would stop reading it. For some unexplained reason he was drawn to see what it was. The smell, in itself, was drawing him to take a look. Such old faded paper caused his interest to peak beyond his control. It was THE GIFT Susan had placed there before leaving town. He opened it and began to read. It was not titled to anyone in particular, so he felt at ease reading, until he reached the words,

'If you do not go within, you go without'

Those words affected him as if lights were turned on. He had long known of this concept, but never had the words been phrased quite this way. He also knew he had requested a situation in his life be changed but he knew not from where the answers were to come. He read and re-read it over and over. He felt the answers were coming quicker with each reading. In fact they were coming clearer, and in a strange way, he felt they were directed at him personally. She would not be able to use it tonight, so his passion for THE GIFT allowed him to justify taking it home.

The next morning he arrived extremely early. Nicole looked so much better he thought. Maybe it was because her color had returned to her face and once again he saw the glow he had grown so accustomed to seeing. He went down to the cafeteria and brought back a cup of black coffee while he read THE GIFT another time. Before he could finish, he was startled as a man walked in and surprised him at the early hour.

"Excuse me!" the man said. "Are you the doctor?"

"No, I thought you might be the doctor. I'm Nicholas Andrews, and you are?" he said extending his hand.

"I'm Joe Butler, her step father. The hospital called last night, told me there was no need in coming over, she was heavily sedated and that someone was already with her. I guess it must have been you?" Joe said, he knew from Susan that

Nicholas owned the store chain.

"Yes, it was my store where she was hurt and I feel dreadful," Nicholas came back sensing Joe was already aware of the circumstances.

"Susan has told me Nicole met you at a party. You should not take these things personally. That's why they call them accidents." The non-judgmental way Joe talked gave Nicholas relief from the obvious tension he was feeling.

"How's she doing?" Joe inquired "Her mother called last night and is taking the first flight she can get home."

"Well, she looks a lot better than she did yesterday. To be honest, she scared the hell out of me for awhile." Nicholas answered, as he placed THE GIFT back in his coat pocket. "Well, I've got to go," he said "I've not been back at the store since yesterday and you need some time to visit with her. It was nice meeting you." Nicholas walked out the door.

The problems of the Grand Opening were waiting on him when he arrived at the store. The manager was obviously in great remorse about what had happened. Nicholas, who was prepared to give him the riot act, remembered Joe's words as Phil Hudgins, the manager, approached....

"Accidents happen Phil, I understand. I don't expect such total disregard of my wishes will become a habit, but I understand. Let's just put this one behind us, okay?" Nicholas said.

The manager saw an immediate change in Nicholas. He was expecting to be fired on the spot, and this sudden change in his personality was welcomed. This did make him cautious of what might come next, not understanding Nicholas' attitude. He was not the only one to notice the changes had taken place, everyone saw a new man in Nicholas. The sharpness of his commands had been smoothed away, his smile was much more genuine, and the look he displayed was more like that of someone in love. In fact, it was just the case. The personal situation that had bothered him was his total rejection that he needed anyone to share his life. Nicole had come as a whirlwind, swept him off his feet, and now look what had happened. He concentrated on going within and was prepared to deal with the results. For whatever strange reason, Nicholas felt extremely positive on both meeting Nicole and being exposed to THE GIFT.

For whatever reason, Nicholas knew some major changes had happened in his life. It was not all Nicole that brought them about. There was something else, a newness of spirit, a refreshing change that seemed to take away some of the bitterness inside him. He knew it was only the start of more to come, and there was no fear.

THE APOLOGY

Joe met Susan's flight, which was late as usual. She too had felt a barrage of mixed emotions. She was just getting to know Nicole. She was feeling she had pushed her more than she should have. Had she forced her to take THE GIFT against her wishes? What would she find when she got to the hospital? Her life was all she had ever hoped it would be. She had believed she would find the loving husband to share her life, which she had found in Joe. She knew, without a doubt, the business would be a success. She knew she would be happily satisfied, and now this. Joe's touch and warm greeting calmed her down, and she began to think like herself, even with the mother instinct pushing her patience to the limit. She would wait and see for herself what the conditions were before she started to panic.

They went straight to the hospital from the airport. Susan was surprised when she walked into Nicole's room, only to find her in a much better condition than she had pictured in his mind. After being briefed on her condition by the doctors, she went over to the bed, leaned down and kissed Nicole's forehead.

"Nicole, it's Mother. I love you." She said not expecting a reply. Much to her surprise Nicole opened her eyes and with a dry mouth moaned,

"And I love you back," Nicole answered in a faint voice.

It was almost a magic reaction. Susan knew the bonding had returned again. She had taken too much for granted and it had taken a calamity to bring them closer together. Nicole looked up at Susan. There was a freshness in her bruised and bandaged face.

"Mom, I want to tell you something. I think I have fallen in love. I suspected it the first time I met Nicholas, but it was the oddest thing. While I was unconscious, it was his presence I continued to feel. There was much more to it then mere concern. I felt true love there. It might be in the way he called my name. I heard him, but could not answer." Her face was radiant. Susan thought she had read THE GIFT. What else could it be?

"I told you THE GIFT could change your life, silly you didn't want to even consider it." Susan said, knowing she was right all along.

"What gift?" Nicole asked.

"The paper I placed in your purse before I left town. You did read it didn't you?" she asked in surprise.

"Mother, I don't know what you're talking about, I haven't read anything."

"It's in your purse! Besides, I was pushing my luck hoping it was. There is no need to bother you now. Where is it? I'll just take it back." Susan began to relax.

"How would I know? I just woke up. Maybe it's in the closet over there," Nicole pointed.

Susan opened the door, found the purse and, after a minute, frantically began to search.

"It's not here! Did you see it Nikkie?" came her words.

"No, never even opened the thing Mother. Sorry," came Nicole's reply.

"It's gone!" was Susan's only response.

She knew now was not the time to get upset. She could find out later what happened to it, but her expression showed her grave disappointment. Nicole was back; her daughter's return was much better than a silly old piece of paper. But where did it go? It was very important. But she was tired now and wanted only to rest.

"I'm sorry I even tried to force it on you. It's all right and you are safe." Susan sat holding Nicole's hand, and caressing her face until she was sure she was in a peaceful restful sleep.

"I'm worn to a frazzle, and I need to stop by the office and then I want a hot bath and a nap," she whispered to Joe. She leaned down over Nikkie and said, "Looks like my girl will be coming home soon. And, oh, thanks for the ' I love you'." Stopping at the nurse's station, she instructed, " Please call me with the slightest thing you need," she said as they headed out the door.

Later that evening, Nicholas returned to visit Nicole. She was asleep, and he of course had no idea she had come out of the coma. He walked in very quietly, and stood by the bed watching her face intensely.

"Oh, Nicole, you could never have known the fool I have

been. For far too long I have forced out anyone from my life. Until yesterday, I might have gone on with my personal masquerade, but seeing you lifeless made me consider what I might have thrown away. I read the paper in your purse. Forgive me, it fell out. I feel it was almost as if it were intended for me to read. The words seem to be so familiar, and yet completely new to my own self-imposed deafness. I realized, for the first time, I loved someone again. Yes, more than I had loved myself. I've spent my life running away from love, my father seemed to have taken it away when he left, but I realize I love you, please be all right." His words were spoken low as he poured his heart out for the first time in his life.

"Oh God, what have I done? What have I done?" he began to weep as he lay his head next to her on the bed.

She had heard his every word. The tears in her own eyes could not be held back. Slowly one dripped escaping the corner of her eye.
"You've done nothing but be honest," she whispered.

His head jerked with the quickness of surprise. He could not help himself, and stood to his feet and through watered eyes spoke her name, "Nicole."

Her smiling eyes told him her feelings, and he leaned down to her waiting lips. He was almost afraid she was too bruised. She was afraid she was repulsive. But the kiss was the wonderment each of them needed. The seconds that passed somehow told them they had found what they both had been searching for, which had been denied for so long. The tenderness was shared between them; the caring exchanged with the gentle touching which became much more passionate as each second passed. And their quest for love ended at last.

After a few uneasy and somewhat embarrassing moments, they started to grin at each other, knowing what they had found.

"Well, this is the first time I've had to almost die for someone to tell me they loved me," Nicole said with a laugh.

"I have not told anyone those words since long ago when I lived at Whittler's Point," he said.

"Maryland, you lived at Whittler's Point, Maryland?" Nicole asked with her eyes wide open.

"Yes I was raised there," Nicholas replied. "You know where it's at?"

"Why yes, that is where I was raised, in Barne's Bay, just down the road. Then I moved here to Arkansas with my mother. Where did you go to school? We should have known each other."

"I attended private schools, but maybe I have seen you cruising around the Shoney's up there," he replied. "That's why I had the feeling I had known you before." he replied. They talked on remembered things long passed of youth and, with an occasional kiss, enjoyed their newfound love.

The next morning Susan came in early, and was surprised to find an even better Nicole than she had left the night before.

"Well, well, there must have been some magic elf around to make my girl look so radiant this morning," was her first remark.

"Yes, Mother, there has been one particular elf. Nicholas

came in last night I could not believe it, but thinking I was still unconscious, he confessed his love for me. It was wonderful," she said smiling like a Cheshire cat.

"Nicole, I can see by the look on your face this has made you very happy. The nurse told me on the way in here, that we could take you home. The doctor has dismissed you. So, want to get dressed and get the hell out of this place?" Susan asked, knowing what the answer would be.

Susan started packing things up around Nicole's bed, then the closet. When she saw her purse she noticed THE GIFT was partially visible.

"Nicole, here's the thing I mentioned yesterday. Where was it when we looked for it?" Susan asked.

"Oh, Nicholas said it fell out of my purse. He took it home and read it. Hope you don't mind. Guess he put it back in my purse."

Susan saw no harm. No one would really be violating her promise if she did not give it to them. She was just glad to get it back, still sure it was Nicole who was to be the next recipient. She would just learn to be more patient, Nicholas Andrews might just be a passing fancy.

"When am I going to meet Mr. Nicholas Andrews? I'm dying to see just who has had this traumatic effect on your life." Susan said, still searching the room to make sure nothing was left.

"Oh, thanks for reminding me, I need to call the store and leave word I'm going home and won't be here at the hospital." Nicole said.

He was not there. She left a message and they were off for the house. On the way, Susan noticed a complete change in Nicole. She had become a new person talking, not only about Nicholas, but also about the challenges that lay ahead in the job. This was a pleasant change for Susan. She thought THE GIFT could wait, after all it had waited this long. They would discuss Nicholas and this change further when they got Nicole home and settled.

Susan had demanded Nicole stay home from work. There was nothing important enough she would have to attend that couldn't wait. Nicole was anxious to get back, but still felt tired from her experience. She had called Nicholas, and he was going to be out of town for a few days, so introductions to her mother would have to be put on hold. Besides the bruises were as bad as they were going to look and she wanted to look her best when he saw her again. This time could be better used in her own personal thoughts.

The day had started off about the same for Susan. Her brief absence had caused the usual backlog of things that needed to be handled. She was pleasantly surprised to see Katron had called. This return call would be the most pleasant of the day, she thought. There was no answer and she kept the message slip to remind her to keep trying to reach her. It had been so very long, she thought, since she had talked with her. The talks were always welcomed and, in reality, she missed those times so long ago. They had tried to keep in touch, but with all things life threw at her, had widened their distance. However, they never lost their feelings for one another. With the situation with Nicole, she really needed to visit with Katron. She would gather her thoughts as to what direction she needed to go. Katron never gave her the answers directly, but her wisdom was always there to provide just the right guidance.

Susan's schedule was hectic this morning. New products, department meetings, and general catch up chores kept her running. Susan took off time to share lunch with Joe. She had felt a distance growing because of Nicole being there, and she had vowed nothing would ever come between them. He had been the ideal man. Everything she had ever wanted. For that matter, everything had happened to bring about ideal conditions. Her life had turned out just as she had clearly pictured in her mind. The visit with Joe seemed to inspire her and fill the void the pressures of life had drained from her. He always seemed to show her the patience and understanding she needed, and was secure enough in his relationship, her love was all he ever needed. Susan knew she had found everything that had made her life completely whole.

She was exiting the elevator when she ran into Nancy.

"Susan, there's someone in your office to see you. I took the liberty to see what was scheduled for the day and have taken care of everything. I'll take your calls and get the marketing people off their butts and make sure they have everything needed. I don't think they were ready for the meeting today anyway," Nancy said, as she motioned for Susan to get to her office. Susan felt truly blessed to have someone like Nancy who could take control when needed. It was no wonder Nancy had become an officer in the corporation, as well as a sizable stockholder.

Susan opened the huge door to her office wondering who Nancy thought was so important. It was always a quiet door, and she didn't disturb the thoughts of the tall man standing in front of the window, which looked out over downtown Little Rock. As the door shut, the click of the knob snapped him back to reality.

"Damn Nation, a fella could sure nuff get a nose bleed up this high," came his first words as he began to turn around. He no sooner started his turn when Susan recognized him and began her quick steps in his direction.

"Charlie!" she said her friendly tone expressed her surprise and pleasure at seeing him. With a quick hug around his neck, she asked, "Where's Katron?"

"Over there," as he pointed to the farthest corner from the window. "She don't care for heights much." Charlie got what he wanted to say in. He knew that when those two got together he was going to have to whittle or something, cause he always wound up feeling like a fifth wheel.

Susan's walk was much faster over to Katron. With a big smile, and arms extended, they embraced each other with the fondness of sisters. Where Susan had gained a pound, Katron had lost a few pounds from working the garden, canning and the usual chores for the preparation of fall.

"God, I've missed you," Susan said in a loud voice. "No wonder I couldn't reach you at the house. You were on your way here. Why didn't you call?"

"We did, but when I told Charlie I wanted to see you, he moved faster than I give the ole man credit. We were ready to go before I knew it and, you don't keep Charlie waitin long," said Katron as she reached out to hug Susan again, as if she didn't get enough the first time around.

"I'm totally surprised. What on earth was the hurry to come see me? I would have been more prepared for you with a little notice," Susan said.

"Well, I got something for you, but my heart has just longed to see you so much almost any ole excuse would have done the trick. Now, Charlie and I don't want to put you out none so, we need to get us a motel room," Katron said.

"I'll have no part of that idea. I have the guest room, if you can still sleep next to Charlie. Besides Nicole would love to see you. She's back with me you know. I'll have to tell you all about her life, or better yet I'll let her," Susan insisted and immediately picked up the phone and called the house.

She instructed the housekeeper to prepare for two more people, and to get the guest room ready. Katron and Charlie weren't the restaurant types. Susan took off the rest of the day to enjoy her special friends.

Other than the fading blue from the bruises and a small bandage where her head was stitched, Nicole was almost good as new. She was excited to see Katron and Charlie as she too had become quite attached to them. She spent time with them during the summers when she came home to work. She had found the same value in Katron's understanding as Susan. She couldn't wait to tell them about Nicholas Andrews. After all the rest of her news was somewhat bleaker. The reunion was a most pleasant break from the rush of city life, and it was refreshing to renew friendships and remember old times. Ten o'clock came and it was time for Charlie to hit the hay. The long drive had tired he and Katron, so, it was an early night for everyone, except Nicole who was waiting on a call from Nicholas. She couldn't sleep knowing after he returned to town they would talk once more.

The next morning Susan found Charlie and Katron already up, way before the housekeeper came. Katron had made Charlie his morning coffee and they were at the kitchen table, astonished with Susan's home.

"You sure done all right by yourself, Missy," Charlie said. He knew her name, but she enjoyed the nickname he'd given to her. He still got a laugh out of their first meeting by the pond.

"Why thank ya Charlie, I see you've got the coffee made already. Nellie, the maid will be here in a few minutes and she can fix us breakfast," Susan said.

Charlie and Katron just gave each other a surprised look. "You gotta maid now?" asked Charlie.

"Well, she's more than a maid Charlie. We call them.... Hell, don't know what you call 'em, but she cooks, cleans, and does a variety of other chores, and is paid well too," Susan said as she poured herself a cup of coffee. About that time Joe came down to the kitchen.

"Joe, let me call Nancy and have her reschedule your plans for today and you take Charlie over to Mike's pond and let him see how the big fish are caught," Susan said.

"Yeah, Charlie I've got this friend who has stocked his private pond with bass, seven pound minimum, they'll make ya wet your pants when they strike," Joe excitedly said. He enjoyed having Charlie visit. It had been a rough decision to give up his job and position, but the love for Susan he held in his heart made the decision easier, but it was very nice to go fishin with Charlie nonetheless.

Susan knew Joe wanted any excuse to get back to Mike's and it would give her lots of time to visit with Katron with no one else underfoot. Charlie didn't have to be asked but once and it was not long after breakfast the men were gone for the better part of the day.

Susan and Katron dressed and went out for a short shopping spree. Susan just wanted to get Katron something she could take back to "Hooterville" she could treasure and remember her by.

Katron had brought her own tea, and anyway, it was extra special the way Katron made tea, that in itself brought back wonderful memories. They sat in the living room when the conversation got still.

"Well, Katron, you said you had something for me. Still got it?" Susan inquired. There was a strange calm came across Katron's face.

"Yes, Maggie, it's upstairs, I'll go get it." Katron said leaving the room momentarily.

Susan found a bit of pleasure with the sound of being called Maggie, no one but Katron called her that, and it felt nice. Katron returned to the room with an envelope.

"Now, before I give this to ya, I need to tell ya what happened," Katron said, with a more serious tone. "I don't know what's in here," she said, handing the envelope to Susan. A single word was written on the outside, 'NIC'

"I know I wrote it cause I'm the only one who could have. I don't remember getting up that night, but the next morning it was layin on the kitchen table. Charlie didn't put it there. All I know is it might be meant for Nicole," Katron said.

"I just knew it was meant to be Nicole, Katron," Susan

said. "I tried to give THE GIFT to her but she never read it. It was about the same time she had fallen in love with Nicholas Andrews and I thought the timing was wrong to try while her heart is in a spin. I just knew it was meant for her."

"I'm not asking what THE GIFT is," Katron said, "but love is a powerful gift in and of itself. Perhaps now would be the best time to share it with Nicole. With all the decisions they will be making, they may need all the help they can get," Katron said with a smile.

"Yes, you're right, as usual. I want to meet this new man in Nic's life and would like you to share the moment with me. I'll ask her to invite him over for dinner and we can both meet this dream man of Nicole's," Susan said anxious for the evening to come about.

Susan did ask Nicole to have Nicholas come over for dinner. The plans were made for a day away, because of conflicting coordinating schedules. Nicole was on pins and needles wanting everything in the house to be just right. All she could talk about was him. Susan could see his effect on Nicole was powerful and she had second thoughts about giving her THE GIFT. But the night came, and erased all doubts in her mind.

There was not a flaw. Everything was perfect. Flowers were delivered and set the house off with both beauty to the eyes and lovely fragrances to fill the rooms. The meal was extra special and everyone, even Charlie, understood this was going to be Nicole's night. Everyone was in the den when he arrived. Nicole greeted him at the door and took him into the living room for a short visit prior to his meeting the family and friends. She wanted to warn him of the little things he could expect like, looks, remarks and even an occasional stare. Nicholas just laughed at her concern.

"I'm a big boy now Nicole. If they can't tell I'm in love with you, then so be it. If they want me to act in any way differently from what I am, so be that too," he said with a laugh. As he was thinking, Susan appeared in the door.

She was prepared to speak, with the usual greeting she so causally gave everyone she met, yet there he was. She knew in her heart this was someone very dear to Nicole, and honesty must come forth. She was prepared to look upon him with a judgmental eye to see the things Nicole was not seeing. Instead, she was taken aback. Her words began and when he stood, she could not speak. Those eyes looked deeply into her soul, in an all too familiar way. Something was there that gave her an uncomfortable feeling immediately, though she did not know why. She gathered her composure and extended her hand.

"I'm Maggie Bagwell," came the words from her mouth. What? she thought, she must have been around Katron too long. "Excuse me, Maggie was a name I was called a long time ago, I'm Susan, please call me that Nicholas," she said with a surprised look on her face.

It was obvious Nicole was beside herself. He was tall and extremely attractive, and the look of love in his eyes for Nicole was more than obvious. Susan escorted them to the den to meet Joe, Katron and Charlie. After a few moments of conversation, dinner was served. Susan could not help but watch Nicholas all night. She knew there was something about him that was exceptionally different. Yes, he had good looks, was charming, and, in his own way, distant, but there was something else he presented that she could not figure out.

The next morning was Saturday and Charlie was pacing back and fourth anxious to get back home. Visiting with

Katron had been an extremely pleasant experience, and Susan hated to see them leave. After they left, she went into the bedroom, opened the dresser drawer and took out the envelope. As she sat, clutching it in hand, she pondered whether to open and read it's contents. It was marked for someone else and despite her overwhelming curiosity, she let it be. She closed her eyes, and as she had done so many times, pictured the lake, and once again made it tranquil. It seemed as if she had only been there a few minutes, enjoying the peacefulness, when it all was explained to her. Everything she had been given was simply payment for the faith she had, in Michael, in THE GIFT and in herself. At last, in a moment, a clear picture was presented. THE GIFT had manifested itself to her and she was fully aware of its true value and why she had been chosen. It didn't make it any easier to understand. She should have known the reason she was selected by Michael, yet in her heart she didn't wish to know, now it was all too clear.

"WHY?" she yelled and was immediately back to reality. At last, she knew the secret behind THE GIFT and what her purpose had been. For a moment she was unable to move as the tears rolled down her cheeks to the closed lips that were forming a smile.

Nicole heard her mother's voice and, with the loudness, feared something was wrong. When she ran to her door, she found her sitting on the edge of the bed with tears rolling down her face.

"What's wrong? Are you all right?" Nicole asked and noticed the envelope in her hand. There was no response.

"Mother, what's wrong?" she said in a louder voice. Susan's eyes then began to focus and realized for the first time Nicole was standing next to her.

"When will you see Nicholas again?" Susan asked.

"In a few minutes. He's picking me up and we are going to the park. WHY?" Nicole's concern was much more evident.

"I want to see him before you leave. Now, let me freshen up before he arrives." She got up and went to the bathroom.

Nicole had never seen her mother act in such a manner. Short words were just not her style on the worst of days, but she could only assume she was all right. She went back to her room still concerned, but started to get ready for her prince to come to her.

Nicholas was a person who was always on time. Exactly at one o'clock he pulled into the drive in his Mercedes convertible. Nicole was explaining that her mother was acting a bit weird and had requested to see him. Then suddenly, Susan appeared in the doorway. She had done her best to regain her composure, yet there was still a distant look in her eyes. The words she was about to say were a total surprise to the both of them.

"Nicholas," she greeted him, this time not offering her hand. "I know you love Nicole. And it is as it should be. How it was meant to be. However, you have not been totally honest with her or yourself." Susan's eyes told him the seriousness of the situation and the power behind her statement.

Nicholas found himself guilty in his own eyes. For whatever the reason, he knew Susan knew everything about him, and her words began to cause him to become cold and uncomfortable.

"I know this relationship was formulated long ago, but now you must tell Nicole the truth. This is for you," and she handed the envelope to him and walked out of the room.

Nicole just stood with her mouth open. "What's going on Nicholas?" was her only remark.

"Let's just go to the park," he turned and said.

The conversation was very limited as they drove. Nicholas knew, for some reason, what Susan was saying. He tried to gather his thoughts, and wondered how he was going to tell Nicole. He parked the car, went over to her side and opened the door. She could tell something mysterious had taken place between him and her mother, and she was frightened. He took her hand, held it tightly as they walked to the shade of the largest oak tree in the park.

"Nicole, I don't know how your mother knew about the secret of my past, but she does and it's time to be honest with you. My last name is not Andrews. Andrew is my middle name. I took it as my last name. My father's sudden leaving had traumatic effects on me as a teenager. Not only was I rebellious, I was then alone. I wanted nothing to do with him, or his memory. I went to college because mother wanted me to, not for my own benefit. In the process I lost even more of myself. After almost getting expelled, I left to do the only thing I knew at the time, work in a grocery store. It was the only thing I felt truly comfortable with, and knew it would not disappointment me as my father had done. It took several years, until I learned my father had left me a great deal of money. At first, I did not want a penny from him. Eventually I took it, more out of spite then anything, and purchased a small chain of grocery stores here, and started my life over. I was a new person and I chose not to be in any way related to the past. Now it looks like someone knows me better than I even know myself. For some unexplained reason, I know what is in this envelope," he said with tears forming in his eyes.

"Well, the only way to know for sure is to read it," Nicole said.

He turned to her and with a much different manner looked into her eyes and said. "Nicole, I love you. I feel I always have loved you, as hard as that may be to understand. You have been what I have seen when I pictured the person I wanted to love, to spend my life with. For years I have denied the ability to love, even the concept of love, I rejected selfishly, so as not to let anyone ever come into my life. All that has changed now. When I saw you injured and bleeding I knew what I had done to myself and such fear of loss had never gripped me. I won't lose you. Will you marry me?"

"Yes, of course I will, but what about these changes? Are you sure now? Am I the one you love?" she said, pointing to the envelope, " make any difference in the way you feel now or tomorrow?"

"No, but to make you feel secure let me read it," was his reply as he opened the envelope and began to read.

My Dearest Son,

The time has now come to tell you what you need to know. I have hurt so long with the thoughts of what my actions must have put you through. I am sorry. I want you to know first that I loved you with the deepest affection a man could ever have for his child. I will forever.

With the reading of this letter, I know you have also read THE GIFT. It was always my intention that I pass it on to you. At the time you were not ready to receive it and my time was quickly disappearing. I left no explanations. There were really none that could be truly accepted. I was sick, very sick, and with the many wondrous things THE GIFT had given me, I knew I was to be the only one to end my existence. The timing was never right, we don't truly have control of time, but I could not put your mother, your sister or you through the terrible eventuality, which would ultimately come.

I want you to know that on the last day of my life I found true happiness. I had known for the last two years what was in store for me eventually, and by THE GIFT, found the right person for not only myself, but for you also. If I have the right to ask you a favor, it would be to hold Maggie in the loving regard she deserves. I am not sure you will ever realize what a special soul she is. I created all the aspects that were needed to fulfill this, my last wish. You have now found the person I had long wished for you, and your life will now begin anew.

Nic, I can't begin to express my regret for what was done to you. I can only hope you understand I loved you, and that in such love created my last desire. And you should find the happiness I was not allowed. In my mind, I created the perfect person to perform this task. She was entrusted with it not by chance. Thankfully, all worked out as I expected it would, as my faith has never been by chance. I give you, my son, this gift now, for now is the time. It's up to you to take it, use it wisely, and know this was all done for you. Everything you desire is yours, it will come in a matter of time. Understand my love for you will never end. Your father,

Michael

Nicholas reached for Nicole and pulled her close to him. Without a word, and with tears in his eyes, he kissed her lips, never wanting to lose her. The kiss continued more passionately as her response told him of her love. Just then, there was a gust of wind. He unconsciously released the letter and it began to blow away. As it tumbled, it began to disintegrate, like a child's fireworks sparkler, into millions of tiny pieces. It flew with the wind and landed at the feet of an old man. As it landed, it again was together as the page just read. The man leaned down and picked it up. He stood for a moment, a smile on his face, and love in his deep blue eyes, watching the loving couple. He then turned and with a few steps, and like the sparkler, disappeared into thin air, as this moment in time had been drawn to completion for him. A new beginning was now to start.

ABOUT THE AUTHOR

A baby boomer of the mid-forties, Michael Crawford was born in Atlanta, Georgia when it was still considered a small country southern town. At age five, his life was changed with the loss of his mother to T.B., which would have profound effects on his later life. His primary education was first started in the city school system, and later changed to a rural county system when his family moved to the 'country' which is now a suburb of Atlanta. At age sixteen, Michael was critically injured in an automobile accident which also impacted greatly on his later life.

His first attempts at higher education resulted in frustrated disappointments, as did his first marriage. Without a formal education, Michael did what came most naturally to him, deal with people as a sales representative. It appeared extremely rewarding and he was generally among the top sales producers. At what seemed to be the heights of his sales career, and in the realities of a second failed marriage, fate had another plan for Michael. As a result of the automobile accident, some of the blood received from the many transfusions, he was strickened with Porphuria Cutanea Tarda, a rare debilitating blood disorder. Perhaps it was a blessing in disguise.

Having to face and accept life's true situation, and while on disability, Michael returned to college. Although he earned two degrees in Psychology, Cum Laude no less, it did not produce the end result that was desired. He accepted a job with a chemical company, which in truth was a glorified name for a janitorial supply distributor. While working there he saw a need for an innovative safety product. With help from several sources, he invented and began to market a safety slipper for janitors. This endeavor gave him both the money and the time to work on his book. The possibilities of the spiritual determination of the soul that dwells in every individual soon developed.

A MATTER OF TIME was intended to be the first of a three part series of books which capture the imagination of the reader to simply believe that through the power of purest thought, all things are not only possible but probable. Recognizing that we are a special creation with special abilities, the author has conveyed that we were made in the likeness and image of God, yet we are not truly aware of this aspect. As we seek to understand this deity, we have complicated our grasp of the potential of the power granted to this image. Michael Crawford makes it his mission statement to dissect the complexities of man's vast complications of the truth to a simple, direct and understandable picture. This author's unusual style invites the reader to emotionally participate in the unfolding of the simple truths which lie within each soul.

Look for the continuation of this story coming soon in the sequel, From Time…To Time.

It is my sincere desire to be open to the comments, criticism, opinions and suggestions of the readers who have enjoyed my particular style of writing. Therefor, I extend an open invitation for an opening of communication in an effort to create a unique atmosphere between writer and reader. The magnitude of such an undertaking requires commitment on bother our parts. I promise to acknowledge your personal input if you promise to convey it to me. Below are a few questions that have always been floating in the back of my mind from the first words I placed on paper. I would be most appreciative for your personal assistance in providing me with the answers. I look forward to hearing from you and starting what will bloom into a long relationship of understanding.

1. Did the story interest you from the very beginning and continue to capture your interest ( )Yes ( )No

2. Were you able to quickly identify with the characters, their thoughts and/or actions? ( )Yes ( )No

3. As the story line progressed, did you formulate opinions as to what the next action would be? ( )Yes ( )No

4. Was the graphic nature of the sexual content appropriate to the story line? ( )Yes ( )No

5. Did you find that the book was ( )too short ( )too long? Would you recommend this book? ( )Yes ( )No

I am: Female/Male   Divorced/Married/Single

Under 45/Over 45   Employed/Unemployed

Have Children/No Children

Comments:

_____

_____

_____

_____

_____

_____

(Optional)

Name_____

Telephone (   ) _____

Address _____

City_____State ____Zip _____

( ) I would like to be given advanced notie and an opportunity to
purchase a signed copy of the next sequel prior to publishing

Michael Crawford
P.O Box 641
Cashiers, NC 28717